It Happened on Dufferin Terrace

Melanie Robertson-King

King Park Press

Published by King Park Press

Château Frontenac image: Melanie Robertson-King

Winter Couple: Shutterstock, Inc.
(Signed model release on file with Shutterstock, Inc.)

ISBN: 978-0-9953046-7-3

DEDICATION

For Julie. We may never have met in person, but your virtual friendship was amazing. Thank you.

ACKNOWLEDGMENTS

Thanks to everyone who put up with my daft questions during the research of this novel. Without your help, the book would not have come to fruition.

Chris Longmuir, you've been an angel. I've bent your ear more than once asking for help, and sometimes it's been the same questions repeatedly. You've always taken the time to answer them graciously, and offer support.

Huge thanks to my beta-reader, Dorothy Bush. You helped with fuzzy logic, rounding up the plot bunnies that escaped from their warren, and suggestions on alternate wording to eliminate unnecessary repetition. If I've missed any member of my team by name, I apologize.

Special thanks to my husband, Don, who continues to support and encourage me, and provides a shoulder to cry on when things don't go well. He redesigned my website making it mobile-friendly and taken charge on the domestic front giving me time to write.

One

Gare du Palais, Québec City

Spinner suitcase handle in one hand and her wheeled briefcase in the other, Serenity Layne strolled into the concourse of Gare du Palais. Thanks to the passenger service from Montreal delayed by over thirty-minutes, she reached Québec City late. VIA didn't explain the cause. The thirty-five-year-old business consultant prided herself on her timekeeping. Left to her control, she was always punctual.

A line of taxis parked along the curb in front of the station. At least they weren't idling so she didn't need to walk through a cloud of exhaust fumes. Protocol dictated she use the cab at the head of the queue. The trunk popped open as she got nearer. Soon after, the cabbie emerged from the driver's side. "Ou vas tu?"

Wonderful. Her knowledge of French was limited. "Château Frontenac," she said as she climbed into the backseat, hoping she responded correctly.

The force from the lid closing propelled the rear of the car down. Moments later, the driver eased behind the wheel and started the meter. A mixture of old and new buildings whizzed by on both sides as they drove. Some looked like recent construction, but sympathetically designed to fit in with those of a historical age.

One structure in the distance towered over the others. With the exception of the radio tower, the erection resembled the Empire State

1

Building. In spite of its height, on occasion it dropped from view. A humongous cathedral dominated the foreground. Holiday decorations and clapboard huts monopolized a space on the right crowded with people. The taxi driver had to stop many times as shoppers wandered from one side of the street to the other.

This part of the city had a European flavour. Never having been to Europe, this was the appearance she envisioned. After a few more corners, the extent of the vista where the week of seminars would take place filled the windshield. The towers and turrets gave the impression the castle should be on the pages of a fairy tale. Not that Serenity believed in those. Real life was not like that. At least hers wasn't. Growing up in Toronto was far from the idyllic Prince Charming rescuing the damsel in distress.

Even though the hotel loomed in front of them, the operator made another right turn. Again the New York City icon-like structure came into view. The man steered the car around a small common bedecked with evergreen trees adorned with white mini-lights. A horse hitched to a carriage relaxed near the stop sign and another around the corner. Buses queued along the sidewalk offloading tourists.

An archway protected the narrow alley leading to the guest entrance. The cabbie stopped the vehicle and switched off the meter. Wallet out and ready, she withdrew a twenty dollar bill handed the money to the man behind the wheel. "Keep the change."

"Merci, mademoiselle," he replied as he clambered out and hoisted her luggage from the trunk.

By the time she extricated herself from the backseat, her belongings waited on the walkway.

"Bonne journée," the man called as he scrambled back into the driver's seat. Seconds later, he drove away.

A bellman retrieved her bags and took them inside to reception, and she followed.

"Serenity Layne. You have a reservation for me. I'm part of the *Thacker, Price & Associates – jonathans* group. We're hosting meetings here beginning tomorrow."

"Ah, yes. We've put your party in Place d'Armes for your symposium. Just over there if you want to inspect the room while I complete your registration."

The conference room was off the foyer, tastefully decorated and more than adequate space-wise. A wireless BenQ projector sat in the middle of the table. The proposal she conceived depended on PowerPoint slides so the piece of audio/visual equipment was imperative. A retractable screen swayed from the ceiling at one end of the room.

Most hotels offered photocopying services but in black and white. Prior to departing from Montreal, she found a copy shop and printed the documents in colour from her thumb drive. Each of the managers would receive one to accompany the electronic version. Tall panes overlooked the square. The same horse and coach lingered across the street. A cab was now pulled to the curb in front of it.

The red-roofed 1640 bistro on the other side of the green space beckoned. Although the high-end establishment had a range of restaurants, that's where she would have supper. She left the boardroom and returned to the lobby.

"Your baggage has been taken to your room," the girl at check-in said. "Here is your key. I wrote your room number inside the folder. The elevators are just there. Enjoy your stay. Should you need anything, don't hesitate to contact us."

Appreciation nodded, Serenity walked to the bank of shiny doors. While she passed the time, she opened the cardholder and looked up the information.

The bellman left her luggage in the closet space by the door. The lamps turned on, but he was nowhere in sight. The man deserved a tip but now or when she checked out? He might not be on duty if she put it off.

Leather cross body bag discarded on the bed; her coat close behind. A small desk stood along the far wall next to the window. The drawn shades offered no clue to the view from this room. River or city? The warren of corridors in the building made it difficult to determine. Blinds elevated, the vista consisted of the edifice opposite reception. Most of her time would be used preparing for meetings or sleeping so what was visible from her window was unimportant.

Freshened up, Serenity made her way across the quadrant to the 1640 restaurant. Darker than when she got there in the taxi, the illuminations in the trees and on the buildings showed up much better.

The bistro was bustling, but she procured a table without booking in advance. After perusing the menu, she decided on the cheese and cold cuts plank for one and a pot of green tea. The local cheeses included ranged from hard cheddar to creamy Brie. The meats finished the meal to perfection.

By the time she got through her feast and left the eatery, night had fallen. The wind had strengthened while she was indoors. Now her hair whipped across her face. An errant shock tucked behind her ear, she took her beret out of her coat pocket. Once on her head, she pushed her ash blonde tresses inside.

The promenade overlooking the water looked inviting. Hands rammed deep into her pockets; she wandered over that way. Lights on the opposite shore sparkled and danced in various colours on the dark water. The damp night air chilled her to the bone, so she returned to her room.

After tossing her hard-shell on the bed, she removed her toiletries and flannel pyjamas, and completed her bedtime ablutions. She pulled back the covers and crawled into the cozy bed.

The following morning, six months of gruelling work came to fruition. In the Place d'Armes conference room, Serenity turned on her MacBook Air with the PowerPoint presentation and ensured the projector functioned. In addition to the electronic copy, the hard copies she made in Montreal for the *jonathans* participants were placed them in front of each chair.

This was the first time her superior sat in on one of her meetings, making her more nervous than normal. Did he not trust her judgement?

Scheduled to start at ten a.m., a number of attendees were still missing. The time function on her Fitbit indicated three minutes to go. The managers had to arrive soon or her boss's trust in her abilities would be shattered. A brief assessment of her leather-bound notebook confirmed the time and date.

Gradually, men in three-piece suits, shirts and ties straggled in. They nodded at her as they took their seats. During her visits to the outlets across Canada, she came together with them. All were friendly and cooperative. Some stores performed well, while others struggled.

The head of *jonathans* made his entrance. Well over six feet in stature, with a stocky frame, his imposing size commanded respect and attention.

"Good morning," she said.

The man acknowledged her with a nod of his head and moved to the head of the table.

Now, she and the other attendees waited for her missing employer and one last *jonathans* employee.

"We'll give them another five minutes then we'll start. In the meantime, feel free to look at the documents in front of you." She lingered by the chair used by the director of the Vancouver location and smiled.

The door burst open, eliminating the opportunity to speak with the gentleman. In the gap stood the man from the Yorkville Avenue outlet, as unkempt as the first time she met him. When he looked up, his eyes bulged, and his jaw dropped. "You're the hard-nosed, jumped up high and mighty who made trouble. You're the reason we're having this powwow," he snapped.

The hairs on the back of her neck bristled. Coat plucked from the rack, she darted out the door putting on the garment on the fly. The man busted her straight away. No way could she head this meeting now. Where was Martin Thacker? He would have stood by her.

She left the hotel, turned right, and scurried through the arched vehicular entryway on Rue Saint Louis. From there, she stumbled to the boardwalk which ran adjacent to the spectacular architecture and overlooked the St. Lawrence River and the town underneath.

Snow, packed down from shovelling and plowing, made the boards slippery. High-heeled shoes were inappropriate for the conditions, but escaping that room was paramount.

Why did she allow that man to antagonize her? Any other time, any other meeting and she would have let comments like his roll off her. This action was out of character.

Struggling to maintain her balance, she picked her way to the hand rail. At least she had gloves in her pockets. After extracting the knitted mittens, she pulled them on her hands and tried to regain her composure so she could go back to the meeting. She would have to create an excuse for her sudden departure.

Arms resting on the bannister, she took in long, slow breaths. Each time she exhaled a puff of steam formed in front of her.

About to go back into the warmth of the hotel's conference room, she let go and turned. A massive black dog charged at her with a man and a boy in pursuit. The ear flaps of the man's trapper hat resembled wings. Stretched out horizontally, how he managed not to take flight astounded her.

"Tori, bad girl. Halt." The man shouted commands to the canine, but the animal was oblivious to them.

Before she had an opportunity to react, the black Lab launched itself in the air and hit her square in the chest knocking her to the ground. The impact sent her eyeglasses flying and they crashed on the granite ledge beneath the handrail. The child dove for them but couldn't get a proper grip. His fingertips brushed the frames and her eyewear skittered away from him on the icy rock and vanished.

Two

Thacker, Price & Associates, Bay Street, Toronto

Six months earlier...

"Argh!" Frustrated over her inability to balance her previous month's expenses Serenity shouted. Each time she came up with a different answer. She snapped her pencil in half, slammed the writing tool on her desk, and threw herself back into her chair. Something simple – had to be. Otherwise the thing would be balanced by now. She took off her cheaters and tossed them aside before propping her elbows on the work surface and massaging her temples.

When that failed to help, she rose and walked to the window. Even on the dullest days, the field of vision from here calmed her. New City Hall with its curved towers stood on the opposite side of the street. Off to the left, through the maze of high rises, Lake Ontario was just visible. More and more of the panorama vanished behind scaffolding and skyscrapers. The recession didn't slow the construction boom along the lakeshore. There would be precious little to see at all if not for *Thacker, Price & Associates* occupying the uppermost floor of the building.

The rain lashed against the glass in the deluge and formed

rivulets which ran down to the sill. Her day started out bad and maintained its downhill progression. On her walk to the subway stop from her condominium on trendy Yorkville Avenue, an expensive SUV sped through a puddle sending a spray of water over her.

A few minutes later than normal, she swooped out the door so didn't have time to go back home and switch into something clean. At least she kept a complete outfit at work in case of an emergency. Given time, she would have taken down the vehicle's plate number, found out the owner's identity and sent them her dry cleaning bill.

She gazed out attempting to clear her mind. The phone chirped its annoying tone. Panic ensued when her boss's name, Martin Thacker, appeared on the screen. "Serenity Layne, how can I help you?" she said, making an effort to remain calm and pleasant.

"Can you come to my office, Ms. Layne? There's something I want to discuss with you."

"Certainly, I'll be right there." Even though her expenses didn't balance, she had until the end of the following week to complete it. Had something gone wrong on her last job? Was she about to receive the golden handshake? That would not happen; she worked too hard to get this close to the top. The glass ceiling broke when she applied for and got the high-position, retail consultant post. Putting her glasses back on, she gathered her notebook, favourite Parker ballpoint, and hurried to Martin Thacker's office.

Before knocking, she smoothed her skirt and braced herself then turned the knob.

"Come in, Ms. Layne. Take a seat," he said, gesturing to one of the black, leather club chairs in front of his massive mahogany desk.

She slipped into one of them and started to elevate her right leg over her left then stopped. The skirt was a bit too short and too much thigh would show. On second thought, she opted to cross her feet at her ankles and sit at a slight angle to his workspace. The trouser suit from before was perfect, but after the dousing she got, was out of the question. The outfit she kept at work needed to be replaced with something less revealing.

"I have an assignment for you, Serenity. Hope you don't mind me calling you by your first name." The man eased his tall frame into the high-backed desk chair.

"No, that's quite alright," she said tugging the hem of her skirt nearer to her knee, uncomfortable with the familiarity.

"Jonathan Drake, the head of the high-end department store chain, *jonathans*, has hired us. An in-depth study on each of his stores requires our expertise." A file folder skimmed across the desk. "To see which outlets are performing, which aren't, and what they need to do to keep the business from failing. As you know, they are over one hundred years old and one of the last family-owned retail empires to survive this long."

She reached for the docket, flipped open the folder and scanned the subject matter.

"A conference call with the is scheduled in the morning at nine-thirty. Next Monday, you'll begin visiting every *jonathans* location country-wide to gain a feel for what changes are needed to reverse the fortunes of the company." Pencil twirling back and forth between his thumbs and forefingers, Martin Thacker reclined.

"Hmm, doesn't give me much time to prepare."

"Do a good job, Serenity, and there could be a raise and promotion in it for you. Perhaps even a partnership." The man rose from his chair.

"I won't let you down, Mr. Thacker." Stomach performing acrobatics, it was impossible to show restraint. She wanted to shout, scream, anything but remain professional. In her boss's office a spectacle of that nature would not be tolerated. Not wanting to embarrass herself, she scooped up the file and her notebook and returned to her own.

Three

Thacker, Price & Associates, Bay Street, Toronto

Back in her space, Serenity leaned against the solid wood door. "Yes, yes, yes," she squealed pumping her fists in the air before twirling and dancing her way to her desk with a broad, cheesy grin pasted on her face. This assignment was monumental. With the incredible opportunity presented to her, she couldn't let the company down.

For the longest time, she daydreamed about her surname on the company's signage. Resigned to the fact hers would never come before her immediate supervisor. Nor would it trump the late Mr. Price's. Still, *Thacker, Price, Layne & Associates* had a great ring. The firm's name, including hers, rolled off the tongue. It took a few long, slow breaths to calm down. Once past her initial giddiness, she opened the browser on her MacBook Air and searched *jonathans*.

The Wikipedia entry stated the family founded the firm and began operations in 1889, trading under the same name as now. The business started as a dry goods outlet selling articles imported from Scotland and England. The principal location in Québec City continued in its original building on Rue Saint-Jean between l'Hôtel Dieu and Couillard. Over the years the company the expanded into neighbouring space.

Now retail stores were in every major metropolis across

Canada from Vancouver to Halifax. Only the provinces of Prince Edward Island and Newfoundland and Labrador remained *jonathans* free zones.

The conglomerate didn't have a webpage. Most businesses had one, whether it was kept up to date or not, was a different thing. The absence of a virtual existence hoisted a huge red flag.

Next, she opened a second tab and searched the client's finances at Dun and Bradstreet. All appeared to be satisfactory as far as their reputation for making timely payments.

Most days, Serenity worked until well after seven o'clock. Today, she had to take her trouser suit to the dry cleaners near her home and pick up a few things at the supermarket. She turned off her MacBook Air and gathered the accoutrements she would need to carry on with her research into *jonathans* from home.

When she squeezed her way into the subway car, it seemed more crowded than usual. Sandwiched between a six-foot-something tall man, and a short, grey-haired, senior with her folding shopping cart, her ankle was hit as people jostled for space. Every time the man moved, the newspaper under his arm smacked her in the head. A draft of stale air flooded the carriage through an open window when the train began to move. Blended with body odour, strong perfume, and the Limburger-y scent of stinky feet, she couldn't breathe.

To take her mind off the smells and assaults on her, en-route to the Bloor-Yonge Station, Serenity churned over concepts to introduce during their conference call. The creation and maintenance of a website topped her series of changes coupled with a social media presence. Whether he agreed with her or not was something else.

An announcement informing of a delay came over the PA as she walked to the platform to catch the connecting subway that would take her to her cleaner's. The hold-up could be as short as five minutes or indefinite so she made her way to the exit closest to Cumberland Street.

At some point when she was in the subterranean cavern, the rain had stopped. The sun reflecting off the plate glass of one of the many high-rises blinded her. She rifled through her handbag for her Oakley sunglasses. Absorbed in finding them, she stepped off the curb. If not for another pedestrian at the crosswalk, she would have walked into the path of the car speeding through the intersection running the red light. A quick glance stolen at her rescuer. Taller than her, slim, and clothed in a navy blue, three-piece suit, he had the appearance of someone who belonged on the pages of a fashion magazine. Trying to remain professional, she mouthed her gratitude.

The man smiled and started across the thoroughfare leaving Serenity behind; her mouth gaped open in awe of what might have happened had he not stopped her.

In the distance, an emergency vehicle siren wailed. Usually, she didn't hear the sound or was so used to it she blocked it out.

Toronto was a perpetual construction zone, so the pungent smell of hot asphalt wafting through the air came as no surprise, same with the pounding racket of a jackhammer. The unpleasant whiff of exhaust fumes mingled with the aromas of cooking food circulating through ventilation systems.

Trundling her computer case down Cumberland Street, with her trouser suit over her arm, Serenity proceeded to the dry cleaner's. Someone advanced wearing baggy jeans, a dark hoodie, head down, and their ball cap on sideways. Cables dangled from his ears to his mobile phone. To avoid the imminent collision, she sidestepped his path and rammed her knee into a fire hydrant.

Four

jonathans, Bloor Street, Toronto

The majority of her work clothes were purchased from the Hudson's Bay Company. Occasionally, a few things at Holt Renfrew but only at the latter during their end of season sales. Now she found herself on Bloor Street opposite one of the stores belonging to the Drake family. People referred to this segment stretching between Yonge Street and Avenue Road as Toronto's Fifth Avenue because of the high-end jewellery and clothing retailers.

jonathans didn't fit in with the image of the golden mile. The building, one of the older structures on the block looked shabby compared to the rest; the window displays while well done, were a period behind the others on the strip. The storefront held no customer appeal – nothing to entice people in off the street like the other stores. Until now, she didn't know this business existed. With no web page, the only way a person would find out about the location was to use the traditional printed telephone directory. How many people did that anymore?

Despite it being a three-way call, not a face-to-face the next morning, Serenity felt more confident meeting someone for the first time when wearing new clothes. After retracting the case's handle, she clutched the leather straps and entered.

The exterior was terrible, and inside was far worse. The apparel on the racks hung in a haphazard fashion. Flashes of various hues littered the floor under empty hangers. Folded sweaters and trousers remained untidy after customers had plundered through them. Observations made as she went, Serenity walked through the main level. In one spot, the floor felt sticky under her feet.

Once she found a clerk, she approached the young girl. "Is the manager in today?"

"Dunno. Only work here. Come in, punch my time card and punch out at the end of my shift."

With a demeanour like that, this girl would never go far in any vocation. "Is this store always such a mess?"

"Most times. Why? You an inspector or somethin'?" Little Miss Attitude fiddled with her hair as she spoke.

While Serenity attempted to extract some useful intelligence from the girl, a man with an unkempt appearance approached. Close-set eyes framed his long, narrow nose. Head balding, what hair remaining was styled into a comb-over. Mid-forties? One side of his shirttail draped over the waistband of his trousers. His tie sported stains from meals and liquids, and his shoes donned splatters of spilt coffee, and who knew what else.

"Excuse me," she called out and walked to him. "I'm looking for the person in charge."

"You found him. What do you want?" The man folded his arms over his chest.

If this was an intimidation tactic, it was not going to work. "I wanted to talk to you about the condition of this store."

"What business is it of yours?"

The manager couldn't discover, at least not yet, she held a position with the firm hired to perform the consultancy. "I was in the neighbourhood. Never been in before so I thought, why not? The window displays really should be updated." She stopped before saying anything more. Too much talk like that, and he would know something was up.

"All the other stores on the street are a season ahead of you. The intention was to come in and browse for some new work clothes. Now I wish I hadn't. This place is dirty, the displays are a mess, and clothing is on the floor under the racks. Look, I'm doing you a favour by mentioning this. Tidy the place up, inside and out, and you'll be able to compete." Worried she went too far with her last statement she chewed her bottom lip.

"Look, lady, I don't need some jumped up, high and mighty coming in here and telling me how to run my store." The man snatched her by the arm and escorted her to the exit. "Now, get out." He opened the door and propelled her through the portal.

Self control waning, Serenity grit her teeth and took a in deep breath. The man deserved a comeuppance, but she couldn't give it to him here. That would jeopardize the *jonathans* contract so she kept silent. The run-in would be documented later while her supper cooked.

Five

Serenity's condo, Yorkville Avenue, Toronto

Shoes kicked off and keys discarded in the in the bowl on the sideboard, Serenity pulled her rolling case into the dining room. After removing her MacBook and notebook, she went to the kitchen and peered into the fridge.

Cooking for one was such a bore. Nothing in it appealed to her. Quite often, she put in her weekends preparing, packaging individual meals, and freezing them, something she hadn't done in some time. Serenity padded off to the closet where her washer, dryer and small chest freezer were installed, and raised the lid on the latter. Mother Hubbard's cupboard contained more to eat.

A stop at the grocer's around the corner from her or the Bloor Street Market before returning home was her original idea. Rattled by the encounter with the manager at *jonathans,* she rushed home never giving her food shop a second thought.

Back in the refrigerator, she found the ingredients for a Greek salad, if they were fit for human consumption. The unopened bottle of Lipton Pure Leaf was pulled out and a tumbler poured. Beverage brought through to the table, Serenity sat down, flipped open her journal, and turned on her computer.

While waiting on the device to complete its power up

routine, she sipped her iced tea. How she would write up her statement on the rude man? The thoughts formulated in her mind and she feverishly touch-typed before they vanished.

About an hour later, Serenity wound up her report and saved it. Leaning back in her chair, she sighed. Not bothering to check her mail, she shut down, returned for another glassful then to her soaker tub. A hot bubble bath would put the world to rights.

Six

Thacker, Price & Associates, Bay Street, Toronto

Fingers tapping on the desk's surface to the beat of a classical music piece, Serenity studied her notes written for this morning's conference call. The segment detailing her encounter with the manager at the Bloor Street store made her seethe with anger.

The digital clock read nine twenty-five so she gathered her things and walked with purpose to the boardroom.

Martin Thacker rose when she came into the room. "I trust you're prepared for our three-way with Jonathan Drake."

"Yes," she said slipping into a chair on the opposite side of the enormous table. What she wanted to say was something to the effect *'have I ever let you down'* or *'of course I'm ready. When have I not been?'* but held her tongue.

"Thought we'd do it in here. Less likelihood of being interrupted than in my office."

This room was overkill for a call on speaker phone, but when the slide-sign on the door read occupied, those using the room were not disturbed. The same didn't hold true for either of their offices.

Awards the company won over the years adorned the off-white textured walls. At the far end of the room, a fifty-two-inch plasma television hung from a bracket – a video camera for teleconferencing mounted to it. The black table and high-backed, swivel, leather armchairs seated sixteen people comfortably.

A similar credenza stood along one wall parallel to the table. A pitcher and glassware placed at one end and a Keurig coffee maker at the other. In between, sculptures from local artists added the finishing touches to the look.

The phone resounded and she pressed the switch to activate the speaker function. Her employer interrupted not giving her the opportunity to talk. "Good morning. Martin Thacker here."

"Thacker," an all-business voice answered.

"Allow me to introduce Serenity Layne, the expert designated to your account."

"Hello," she greeted.

"A woman? You assigned a woman to represent the needs of *jonathans*?"

"I assure you, she is our best consultant. I wouldn't have given it to anyone not up to the task."

Heat rushed to her face at her boss's compliment and faith in her. "I have some exciting ideas to bring your business into the twenty-first century so you can compete with the likes of Holt Renfrew, Diesel, Debenhams, and Marks & Spencer just to name a few."

"Wha-wha-what?"

"Over the next few months, I'm going to visit every one of your stores Canada-wide. Get input from the personnel. Find out what works for them. One thing, I must recommend is a presence on the Internet, starting with a webpage. Until yesterday, I didn't know there was a *jonathans* on Bloor Street here in Toronto – and I live in the vicinity. Oh, and that store, I trust the rest aren't in the state of disarray and filth I witnessed there. The place is a disgrace to the family name. My findings are fully documented. I can read my report to you if you like."

"No. No, won't be necessary," the man blustered.

The point of her boss's fine-point scratched on the writing pad as he scribbled something then slid the tablet across the table to Serenity.

She nodded.

"If there's nothing else for today, I say we should bring our chat to an end."

"Goodbye, sir." Far from being a feminist, the pompous, arrogant man's attitude with respect to women bothered her. She would swear the manager of the Bloor Street outlet was related to him, if she didn't know any better.

Call disconnected, they both sighed. "What a demeanour. I know you believe in me Mr. Thacker, but I don't think I can work with Jonathan Drake."

"You'll do just fine. Janice has your itinerary and plane tickets. I know I first told you next Monday, but things have changed and your flight leaves Saturday," he said standing.

That didn't give her much time. "But ...," she protested. "I have a ton of things to do before I go and my expense report for last month isn't balanced yet. It's due next Friday and I need more time to finish."

"Are you telling me you're not up to the task? I can assign the account to one of the other consultants," he said with an arch of his eyebrow.

"Yes, I am." Shoulders pulled back, she bristled at his comment. The last thing she wanted was to lose this assignment to someone else.

"Excellent. Bring me your last month's expense statement, and I'll balance it for you. Go home. Take the time off to prepare. The company car will pick you up and take you to the airport tomorrow," he said as he shuffled his paperwork. "Oh, and would you e-mail me your report on the Toronto store before you leave? I want to know what we're dealing with here."

"As soon as I get back to my desk," she replied picking up her notebook and writing instrument.

Relieved to have the rest of the day off, Serenity sent the file as requested and recorded a new out of office message on her phone. Once she completed those tasks, she set up an electronic memo directing people to contact her peer, Phil Bradford, if they required assistance during her absence.

Seven

Serenity's condo, Yorkville Avenue, Toronto

Back home, Serenity opened the itinerary. The schedule was insane. No one could maintain that pace for any length of time without collapsing from exhaustion. Flying from Toronto to Québec City to devote two weeks in the principal retail location. A reservation had been made for her at the Hôtel du Vieux-Québec adjacent to the head office for the duration of her stay. A King Deluxe with a fireplace, no less. The logic behind the decision to start there, she got, but starting on the west coast and working her way east made more sense.

Still, she couldn't let the agency or herself down. The firm had given her a minimum of fourteen days at each *jonathans* location. That would be just enough time to get a feel for things, not much else. Some of the consultations she did took over a month. With the short time she had, to travel across the country, this wouldn't be as in-depth as she would like. The head of the company begrudged paying this much, and not a dollar more. A positive to starting her consultation in here was she wouldn't have to deal with the manager of the Bloor Street store for six weeks, if at all.

With the lack of lead-time before her journey, she didn't have time to hash out a stratagem with her superior over the approach to use. Not that she was incapable of thinking for herself, but she enjoyed those brainstorming sessions and thought they always brought out the best in her.

The sizeable hard-shell piece of luggage was hauled out of the closet, hoisted on the bed and opened. The smaller carry-on was preferred, but on the road for the better part of six months, using the bigger one was imperative. No guarantee of laundry facilities.

The plush panda her father won at the Canadian National Exhibition, when he secured odd jobs on the midway sat in the tub chair under the window. He lugged the stuffed animal home tucked under one arm. At the time she was a little girl. The bear's left eye was missing, courtesy of Erik, her younger brother. The absent orb replaced by a button sewn on by her mother. She never forgave her sibling for ruining her prized possession.

A rush of unhappy childhood memories flooded back starting with her dad, a work-shy alcoholic, who died the year she started high school of a massive heart attack. Never able to cope with things well, even before his death, her mother threw away most of her time locked in her room watching television. Erik's whereabouts remained unknown. Always a rebellious boy, he caused their mother no end of grief with his actions, the worst of which was stealing to support his drug habit. He put her mother through hell and if she ever clapped eyes on him again, it would be too soon. In her mind, she was an only child.

Attention turned back to packing, Serenity plucked garment laden hangers from her closet and chucked them on the bed. Next, she moved on to her dresser and removed undergarments. Thanks to her lousy aim, the panda ended up wearing panties on its head. Giggle suppressed, she snatched her underwear, and waggled her finger at the teddy bear and ordered, "No wild parties while I'm away."

The blast of a car horn jolted her awake. Alarm clock – not set the night before. She leapt out of bed and raced around her condo, a brush pulled through her hair as she went. No time to do it now, her makeup could be applied in the car.

Luggage in one hand, she swung the cross-body leather purse strap over her shoulder. After one last inspection to ensure everything was turned off, she seized her laptop bag and scurried out the door.

With skillful driving on the chauffeur's part, she breezed into Pearson in time to check in and arrive at her gate.

Onboard the aircraft, she removed her MacBook Air and files from her case and stowed the latter on the floor in front of her. Being a short flight, she chose a window seat to work without interruptions when someone had to use the toilet.

So engrossed in reading and typing notes into her computer, she didn't hear the announcement the plane was on final approach for the airport. Not until an attendant came along and told her she had to pack things up, did she feel the increase in pressure. The landing was the only thing she detested about flying. Not hitting the tarmac with a thud, but the increasing pain in her ears.

Safely on the ground and checked bags collected, Serenity made her way to the arrivals hall, where a man stood with a sign emblazoned with her name. She approached him. Once ensconced in the back seat of the limousine, she pulled out the paperwork again and read more.

Extraneous distractions tuned out, she concentrated on the job at hand. Until he announced they had reached their destination, she never lifted her head.

Files stuffed back in her briefcase, she climbed out of the vehicle. Across the street stood the primary location of the *jonathans* empire. The three-storey structure behind her would be her home while she was on assignment in the city. The chauffeur removed her large bag from the trunk and extended the handle.

Now, getting checked in was her number one priority; the store visit after that.

The room was spacious and had an exposed stonework wall. With Wi-fi, a desk, seating area and a flat screen TV that had to be forty-two-inches wide affixed over the hearth, she had everything she needed.

Suitcase hoisted on the bed and opened, she hung her

trouser suits, blouses and skirts in the small closet. An ironing board and iron were provided.

After extracting the telescoping handle of her rolling computer case to its full height, she started for the shop. Vehicles sped by on the central thoroughfare. At least she could enter *jonathans* from the side street where the limo driver stopped the car.

"I'm looking for Jonathan Drake. Would he be in?" she asked a clerk in ladies' apparel.

"The offices are on the top floor. The elevator is through there." The woman responded.

"Thanks."

The location divulged, Serenity found the lift.

Cubicle-filled office area greeted her when the doors opened. Individual workspaces lined the distant wall. To her right, a reception desk. The place was deserted. Then she clued in – Saturday.

A man's voice drifted from the far end of the space so she moved closer to the sound. Light filtered under a closed door. The nearer she got, the louder the one-sided dialogue became. Call ended, she knocked and crept in. "Serenity Layne from Thacker, Price & Associates."

Within minutes, he rounded the desk stood in front of her. The man was huge – tall, stocky, and bald. Crow's feet created deep chasms at the outer corners of his eyes. Other lines formed at the edge of his mouth.

"Ah, you're here, Miss Layne. I trust you had a pleasant flight and your room at the hotel is satisfactory?"

"Yes to both. I want to make a start since I only have a short time here before I fly to Vancouver."

Hand placed on the small of Serenity's back he guided her to an empty office. "This is yours for the duration of your stay here."

After expressing her gratitude, she said, "I'll require a Wi-fi connection so I'll need the password."

"We're not running a wireless network here. Strictly wired. IT will set you up on Monday morning."

That was the last thing Serenity wanted to hear. The more

she accomplished straight away, the better. Without access to their databases, her stratagem needed revision. "One more thing. Are you open tomorrow? I would like to get as much done as I can."

"Yes. Much to my chagrin, we do business seven days a week. Now our hours are shorter on Sundays, but as long as you're out by closing time, you're more than welcome to work weekends. No office workers to help you so time spent on other areas of your study would be prudent."

After he left, Serenity reached for the light switch. The fluorescent fixture hummed – no buzzed like an angry swarm of bees – was more appropriate with its volume. One of the tubes flickered from dark grey to white and back again struggling to come to life.

The office was functional but much smaller than the one she had at the firm. Still, she would make do. No choice in the matter. The lightweight MacBook Air and the files she studied on the flight and in the limo extracted from her bag were placed on the desk. Where to start? From a financial aspect, everything was acceptable. Poring over those documents again was a waste of time. Time better utilized on something else.

Without accessibility to their network until Monday, much of what she wanted to do was put on hold. Journal and favourite ballpoint in her hand, she returned to ladies' wear. "I need your input. What improvements slash additions would you like to see implemented?"

"An updated computer system. This one locks up constantly," said a woman likely in her mid-forties.

"Online buying," replied the young girl, possibly in her early twenties, who told Serenity the location of the offices.

Their concerns noted. Now with representation from two age groups in women's clothing, she needed to find someone near retirement. "Appreciate it, ladies. Is there anyone older. I want to cover all ages."

"Maureen in lingerie has been here for eons," said the younger of the two women.

"Is she working today?"

"Claire, is Maureen here?"

"No. Doesn't work weekends. You won't be able to get any input from her until Monday."

"What about men? Is there a decent demographical representation in sales?"

Assured there were, Serenity went off in search of them to repeat her questions. The consensus was the same as in ladies' wear. Update the computer system and have a secure website. The men didn't appear fussed over the virtual buying aspect but agreed about a computer-generated presence.

The variety and quality of the merchandise from the fashion departments, footwear, and housewares pleased everyone. In the brief walk around getting a feel for the store and the demands of the work force, Serenity was impressed, too. Prior to returning to her temporary workspace, she talked with every salesperson working.

From the people she spoke with on this swing through the flagship *jonathans* location, IT was the bane of everyone. Again, they were a Monday to Friday group, so she could not hear their side of things. Only if the computers went down, would one of them put in an appearance.

Why not Wi-fi? The head office encompassed more than one building, so the firewalls between them were rock as well. Without realizing it, she answered her question. A scribbled note reminded her to inquire about the network infrastructure in the other cities when she visited.

Upstairs in her office, she transcribed her notes. Information technology was the foundation on which she would build her study.

In her room where she had Wi-fi, Serenity emailed her Martin Thacker. While she awaited his reply, ordered something to eat from room service.

Not impressed with the schedule implemented for this consultation, the least he could have done, or had Janice do, was book her on a Sunday flight. Only waste a partial day before she could speak to the IT department.

With mounds of paperwork and costing to investigate, she would have plenty to do and could work from her room. No time for sightseeing anyway, regardless of the weather.

Later that night, about to settle under the covers, a thunderstorm formed in the distance. Low rumbles grew louder as the inclement conditions advanced. If there was a light show to see, she wanted the full effect, not what filtered through the gap in the drapes. Curtains opened she climbed into bed.

At times, the storm sounded like it were directly overhead. Brilliant flashes of lightning streaked across the sky. Rain pelted the window, first, at random intervals then harder. The deluge came down as hard as Niagara Falls tumbling over the precipice.

The following morning dawned dull, gloomy and rainy.

Showered and dressed, she went downstairs to the coffeehouse. The choices included croissants, local jams and other pastries. The wide variety on the morning meal buffet made it difficult select. In the end she decided on crêpes with pure Québec maple syrup and an espresso.

Hunger satisfied, Serenity went back to her room, turned on her laptop, and opened the file folders on her desk. The cross-referencing of the paper files to the ones on her computer took the entire day. With the hotel's Wi-fi, she accessed *Thacker, Price & Associates* so she could retrieve data from her jobs located on their servers.

Once she found the information she sought, she copied it to her MacBook. This was vital to her meeting with *jonathans* IT personnel the next morning. Necessary files downloaded, she logged out. She could log in again if she needed others.

On Monday morning, Serenity took advantage of the coffee maker in her room and the continental breakfast basket. After eating and packing up her briefcase, she pulled the curtains shut and took a shower. When scrubbed she walked out of the washroom swaddled in a thick towel.

At least this morning, the sun shone bright, and the blue sky was cloudless. A short perusal of the weather app on her phone revealed the day would remain clear with low humidity and temperatures in the mid-twenties Celsius.

Armed with this knowledge, Serenity chose a long-sleeved white blouse, black pin-striped pencil skirt, and her red pumps.

Once in her workspace, she wrestled the moleskin and ballpoint from her rolling bag, and introduced herself to the administration staff. Social niceties out of the way, she asked them for the items on their request lists. Again, IT issues topped the lineup. This time, she got different responses, too. The ladies' room demanded repairs. HVAC system required work. Better lighting in the workspaces and corridors.

The information technology department resided in the basement. A well-known fact computers operated best in a chilly environment, but this was beyond cool. This was damp. The overhead maze of ductwork, hanging fluorescent fixtures, water and sewer pipes produced an obstacle course. Light emanated from the far end of the dungeon and she headed for it. In here it was bright, high ceilinged, and warmer than the dark, dank place she traversed.

"Hi, I'm Serenity Layne."

"You're the one they told us was coming to do an efficiency study."

"Yes, but more than just productivity and don't worry, your jobs are safe. That's not what this is all about."

"Yeah right," one of the men clad in a plaid, short-sleeved shirt and beige cargo pants said as he turned around.

The man was lanky, and moustached. Red tinges infiltrated his facial hair, but he was blonde.

"I'm Frank. This is Derek," he introduced his colleague.

As tall and thin as this man was, the other was short and stocky. An odd team for sure. The comic strip characters Mutt and Jeff came to mind, but Serenity managed not to laugh. "So, only the two of you?"

"No. There's Yvan, but he's on holidays, the lucky sod. Gone to Iceland," said Derek.

"You sound jealous."

"Nah, but it sure is a pain in the neck being down to just the two of us."

"Then you're not going to like what I'm about to tell you. Go on, sit down."

The men plummeted to their chairs and stared at her. Derek's mouth hung open.

"At the head of the wish list of everyone I've spoken to is an updated computer system. They claim this one locks up frequently."

"If the old man opened his wallet and sprang for up-to-date equipment, we wouldn't have this problem," said Frank.

"Interesting. You have a wired network here. Have you thought of installing a wireless one?"

"Lady, the walls are stone. Some of them are three feet thick. Wi-fi can't penetrate that."

"Okay, I get it. I'm sure you feel like you're working in the dungeon down here. You need better offices than this."

"Got that right."

Overall, the guys were all right and had every right to be suspicious of her and why she was there. She needed to gain their trust.

"What if I can convince Mr. Drake to spring for a new computer system? Means you two will have to help me with the costing. Do you look after the IT requirements for all the locations countrywide?"

Raucous laughter ensued which answered her question.

"How can a chain of department stores operate like this? What about inventory? How does anyone know when to re-order stock?"

"They use AccPac for accounting and this store only. The others send their sales by courier weekly."

Serenity uttered an expletive under her breath. How could a business function with such an antiquated system? Still, *jonathans* seemed to manage and with no obvious problems. Their credit rating maintained its favourable status.

"This has been an enlightening chat. What time are you off?"

"Five," said Frank.

"I'm staying across the street. I'll buy you each a beer after work. How's that?"

"Great. Sounds like a plan," they said in unison; broad smiles on their faces.

She left the relative comfort of their lair and returned to her workspace. When she arrived on the uppermost floor, Serenity was fuming. Not waiting to be invited, she stormed into Jonathan Drake's office and slammed the door. "What in heaven's name are you thinking keeping those men in the cellar? For one thing, the working conditions are deplorable. Unsafe. If a fire broke out, they would never escape. Not only that, it has to be illegal. That's foremost on my series of changes." She turned on her heel, marched out, slamming the door again, hard enough to make the glass rattle.

Heads raised and wide eyes stared at her. Obviously, no one ever challenged the man, much less a woman. Little did he know, Serenity Layne was a force with whom to be reckoned.

By the time she reached her temporary home, she had calmed somewhat. She picked up her iPhone and called Martin Thacker. After relaying today's experience with the two overworked, under-appreciated technical support workers, she ended with her dressing down of the client. The latter, she anticipated losing her job over. Relief washed over her to hear otherwise.

"He's a hard nut and old-school. The firm has your back no matter what he says. Sorry I missed witnessing you in action, though."

Serenity sighed. Not about to take up with the ranks of the unemployed, and her boss retained his sense of humour.

"Sounds like you're not the only one having a bad day. Phil started in at the Bloor Street store."

"And?"

"The manager is every bit as arrogant and obstinate as when you had your encounter."

"Poor guy. I'll touch base with him later. Commiserate with him. Oh, and I'm taking two of the three IT guys for a drink after work. The third has escaped to Iceland for a vacation, the lucky fellow. Well, I'll contact you again soon." She disconnected the call without giving the man the opportunity to get a word in otherwise.

The entire time she was downs in the dungeon, she scribbled notes in her book. Those points had to be transcribed while she could still read her handwriting, and she had still not spoken with the woman from ladies' wear. Serenity packed up her things and left the office. Her collar was limp and sweat formed on the base of her neck at the hairline. She needed a shower and clean clothes before meeting Frank and Derek. Even a consultation with Maureen was better suspended until the next day when she was refreshed and professional.

Handwritten notes typed along with references to things to investigate, she powered down her computer. The hot spray calmed Serenity's frazzled nerves. Bedecked in jeans, white t-shirt and a blue velvet blazer, she collected her journal and writing instrument and jammed them back in her cross-body bag.

At four forty-five, she went downstairs to be there for the men's arrival.

On their entrance, Serenity stood and waved them to the corner near the inglenook. She sat on an upholstered love seat across from two identical armchairs. A coffee table occupied the space between the soft furnishings. A waitress from the bistro came and took their order.

Beverages in front of them, Serenity started with small talk to make them feel at ease. Soon they laughed and had a great time. "I tore a strip off your boss over your less than humane working conditions."

Their faces paled.

"Don't worry. You won't lose your jobs. I'll see to it. Over the next six months I'll be visiting every store in the *jonathans* empire." Two she wouldn't visit but they didn't need to know about that. "I see a central computer with accounting, inventory tracking and other business-related software installed. All stores, Canada-wide, will be connected."

Their eyes widened. "Won't work. Not with the antiquated architecture we have now," said Frank.

"J.D. will never spring for that kind of system," Derek added.

"He has no choice if he wants his business to remain successful. He'll have to open his wallet. The more capital expenditures he has, the better come tax time."

The guys might geniuses when it came to computers but not so much on the financial side of things. At least not this much.

Serenity took a mouthful of her Coke and returned the glass to the table. "Another thing you'll be responsible for is creating a website."

"The old man will flip," said Derek. "Can see him now, eyes bulging out of his head, face going all red. He'll keel over dead."

She smiled at the vision. "It has to accommodate electronic purchasing."

"You got ba ...," Frank started but stopped.

"Yes, I do." Serenity knew what he was about to say before he clammed up. "And social media, too. Facebook, Instagram, Twitter, Pinterest."

"Love to be a bug on the wall when you lay that on him." Derek bent forward in his seat and took a slug of his beer.

"From what I can see since attaining this contract, a few of the stores have crafted blogs to put the name out there, but nothing is uniform. It needs to be done from a central location. One site, one team to maintain it. Don't forget; I'll be visiting each location over the next few months, getting everyone committed to these philosophies, and more. So what say you, gents? Onwards and upwards?" She stood and raised her glass. The men joined her and toasted their future working with each other.

After they parted company, Serenity ordered room service for her supper. Bedtime came and she embraced it. Her sleep was restless. She could not shut her mind down. Adrenalin coursed through her body from the excitement over her ideas. The night was spent tossing and turning and watching the glowing red digital numbers change on the bedside alarm clock.

After her sleepless night, any hassles from Jonathan Drake were not invited. Although she expected something to happen today, nothing did. She spoke with Maureen. Bless her, all she wanted was an improved changing room where she could fit women for their bras.

"Nothing else?"

"No. That's all." The woman nudged her black rimmed, cat's eye glasses up her nose. "There isn't enough room to swing a cat in any of the stalls, not to mention we need real doors, not just flimsy curtains."

Serenity noted the woman's concerns in her leather-bound notebook. "Can you show me what you now have?"

Maureen guided the way to the back corner of her division. Drapes, or what passed as them, separated the fitting rooms from the open floor area, the section bordered on being as nasty as IT in the basement.

"So, in place of eight cubicles, cut back to a maximum of six? Take some space from your department and put up a wall with a doorway leading into it. Install secure doors with locks."

"Could you arrange that? You would make an old woman extremely happy." She fussed over a selection of bras on plastic hangers causing them to chatter against one another.

"Thanks, Maureen. Your concerns are in my proposition." Expanding the dressing rooms and making the individual stalls private was an easy fix compared to some of the others.

Serenity returned to her office and added the woman's desires to her burgeoning spreadsheet of requests.

Frank blew in after lunch. He connected her to the in-house computer system and provided her with the password.

"I'll also need access to the accounting software."

He obliged and soon had her hooked up. "AP, AR, Employee database. Just names, addresses and phone numbers. Payroll is outsourced. No Internet access."

"Is there such a thing as a boardroom in this place?"

He chuckled. "Nah. Years ago. You're in it."

His comment stunned her. This tiny office was a

conference room at one time? What was the phrase Maureen used to describe her changing rooms? Ditto for here. How the business functioned amazed her. No contact with the outside world except via their cell phones and on their breaks. Mind you, that did keep productivity up.

With the passwords written in her moleskin, she closed the book and put it in her handbag.

"If there's nothing else," said Frank, "I'll head back to the dungeon."

"Can you and Derek come up for a chat? Say two o'clock or so?"

"Unless the whole system crashes."

"Great, I'll see you then." Serenity stood and walked out with him. She stopped at the receptionist's desk. "They tell me you no longer have boardroom. What about a whiteboard and markers, or at the very least and easel and writing pad?"

"I'll look. When do you need them?"

"An hour from now."

The expression on the girl's face said she found her demanding. A few unsavoury words accompanied her thoughts.

She returned to her office. Should Giselle source the requested objects, she would bring them to her.

The men crossed the threshold as the receptionist brought in an aluminum stand with a jumbo pad of thick paper and some coloured markers. Not ideal, but they would work.

Serenity outlined a circle in the middle of the sheet. "This is here. The hub." A series of lines spread out from the centre and smaller round shapes at the ends of them. "These are the rest of the stores. Connect them to us."

By the time they stopped, markings in red, blue, green and black covered the page. Some were solid, others dotted. The newsprint looked a mess, but they knew what each line and tint meant. "Okay, you're the IT experts. Take this and figure out what's required to bring it together."

Enthusiasm gushed from them. After the two left, she collapsed into her chair. Their brainstorming get-together went better than she expected. Give a computer geek a next to impossible project, and they'll prove you wrong every time.

Out of habit, Serenity opened the browser on her MacBook only to receive an error message. No connectivity was an immense pain in addition to inconvenience. She reached for her smartphone.

The web was accessible on the tiny screen. She scrolled through the settings and discovered mobile hotspot and connected her device through her phone's 4G. She was hooked into the world beyond the confines of the business without having to wait to go back across the road. Signal weak, it was slow and dropped out.

Derek said the stone and her office was in the middle of the uppermost floor with no windows. What about the Interac machines? They all worked. Telephone lines. They didn't depend on the Internet, but Ma Bell instead or whatever company *jonathans* used.

When Serenity checked in, two boardrooms were off to the side – a small one and a larger one. The place had Wi-fi. If no one booked either room …, her imagination started to run riot. She packed up her things and went to the hotel.

In luck, the smaller one was available, and she was welcome to use its facilities. It was comfortable and nearby a system failure required attention.

The majority of her plans for *jonathans* necessitated technical help, so she didn't see a problem with whisking the IT people across the street. Still, she needed Jonathan Drake's blessings. After she gave him a dressing down, he might not be so amenable to her dragging his staff offsite.

She returned to big man's office. "For the next couple of days, Frank and Derek will be joining me in the conference room at my hotel. With your antiquated computer system and absence of Internet, it's impossible to hold a meaningful meeting. Before you panic, we're only over the road and if anything happens, they can be reached by phone." Serenity backed away from his desk and turned. "So that's a yes then."

Next, she descended to the bowels of hell and informed the guys. "Bring that fabulous scribbled on paper with you, too. We've got lots to work on."

"But …"

"Cleared with the man upstairs. Now, you're a phone call away. Further, if you crack your head on something or trip up the steps. Some fresh air and sunshine wouldn't go amiss. Who knows you might even get rid of your prison pallor."

The remainder of this week and all the next, Serenity worked closely with the two men on the blueprints for a countrywide grid.

She ensured they both had her email address so they could remain in contact before she left for the airport for her flight to Vancouver.

Eight

Plains of Abraham, Québec City

Roger Scott sauntered across the grass with Tori, his black Lab. Index finger slipped through the ring of the choke chain, he unclipped the tether and nodded to his son. Adam threw the tennis ball with as much strength as a ten-year-old boy could muster. Once the sphere was airborne, he released the dog and she bounded off in pursuit.

Lead gathered, he eased himself to the ground under the shade of a gigantic maple where he could keep an eye on his boy and their retriever. He drew up his knees and rested his arms on them; the dog's rope dangled in front of his legs. A riding lawnmower droned near the Edwin-Bélanger Bandstand.

Another city labourer sauntered by him carrying an idling, gas-powered string trimmer. The sun beating down on the reflective stripes on his bright orange safety vest blinded him, and he shielded his eyes with his hand. The worker squeezed the throttle and the machine roared to life. Grass clippings flew into the air. So much for a quiet day on the Plains of Abraham.

While he relaxed and supervised the sport of fetch, which Tori loved more than anything else, his Samsung S7 vibrated in the holster clipped to his belt. Fumbling with his free hand, Roger plucked out the device to find out who had contacted him. It was an email in reply to an advert he placed on match.com. Only one minor problem, he had never put an ad on any dating site.

Suddenly, he missed his wife more than usual. He still wore his wedding ring; never taken off the platinum band since her death three years ago. In the beginning, he mourned her loss. Then his grief turned to anger. In his mind, she took the coward's way out when she swallowed the bottle of sleeping pills one day when he was at work and Adam at school. He kicked himself for not seeing the signs while there was still time to act. Get Brigitte the help she sorely needed. His young son discovered his mother and called him panicked because he couldn't awaken her. Why couldn't he have found her? Another thing he beat himself up over. A small boy should not have had to endure such a thing.

His phone vibrated a second time. Was one of his workmates pulling a practical joke by putting his profile online? Again in response to another ad but this time on a different website. The note mentioned the photograph of him with his adorable son and gorgeous dog. None of his colleagues had access to any pictures like that. Only the one taken for his ID badge.

"Watch this, Dad," Adam called, tossing the ball straight up in the sky. Tori watched and when it started to descend, leapt into the air and clamped her mouth around the orb.

An idea came to him. What if his son did it? He wouldn't, would he? That would explain the picture. The longer he sat and stewed over it, the angrier he got. "Come on you two. Time we headed back home."

"But Dad, we just got here."

Getting to his feet, Roger went on, "I said time to go home. No arguments. We're going home. End of." He clipped the leash to Tori's collar, and they returned to their house.

On their walk from the Plains of Abraham to their home on Rue des Remparts, overlooking the rooftops of the town below, his smartphone never stopped vibrating.

Nine

Roger's Home, Rue des Remparts, Québec City

When Roger opened the front door, Adam lunged inside and darted up the stairs to his room. If that didn't say guilty, he didn't know what did.

Tori's restraints removed, he hung them on their hook mounted on the wall. The dog trotted to her bed beneath the window, walked in circles one way, then reversed before lying down with a thud.

Roger started for the staircase but hesitated at the bottom. Serious thought was needed on how to approach the subject. Adam was seven when his mother passed away – old enough to remember her and still miss her. That might be the way to go. Find out if his son had played matchmaker on the two dating sites. Who knew how many others had his personal information plastered all over them?

His Samsung buzzed so many times; there barely a pause between rings. He took the device out of the holster and left the cell phone on the table in the foyer. Interruptions during what would be a serious conversation with his son weren't needed.

"Hey, buddy. Mind if I come in?" he said turning the

knob.

Adam hunkered cross-legged on the mattress, elbows on his knees, and his chin in his hands. The boy looked up and nodded, his eyes red and puffy like he had been crying.

Roger sauntered over to the bed, sat beside him and sighed. "I know you miss your mom. I miss her, too."

"But … I hear you talk about her. You're angry. You swear and say mean things about her."

"I wish she got help. Maybe, if she had, she would still be alive. I'm mad – furious – at her actions. She acted selfishly. Never gave any consideration to ours, her parents', and her siblings' feelings."

"We never see Nana and Pop anymore. They used to come around lots right after mom died. Then they stopped. Why?"

"I can't answer that, son. Possible they thought they were too much of a reminder to us?"

Adam tipped his head on Roger. In seconds, he had his arm around the child. "What would you think if I started seeing other women?" It was out there. The elephant was shrinking from an enormous pachyderm into a smaller, more manageable sized invisible third party.

The boy raised his head. "Dating?"

"Sure. Doesn't mean I don't love your mom or think about her." He hugged Adam. "So," he drew out the word before continuing. "Is that why you started a profile for me on the two dating sites?"

"More than two," he mumbled, hanging his head.

"How many then?"

"Many as I could." He faced his father.

Roger's stomach lurched. Match and eHarmony were well known. There were more, but could he remove himself? He earned a living as a data security specialist, removing himself from them – a cake walk. The situation more of an embarrassment than anything. The boy's heart was in the right place. He meant well.

With social media, he was a Luddite. His job tied him to a computer all day. Spending his evenings in cyberspace was a waste. Quality time with his son was what counted. Some nights they played Snakes and Ladders, others they participated in sports until bedtime. Night time sporting events were postponed until the weekend when they didn't have to get up the next morning for school or work.

"Can I ask you a question?"

Adam nodded.

"Why did you do it?"

"Because you're always sad. I thought if you found someone you'd be happy again."

A ten-year old's wisdom.

He ruffled his son's hair as he stood. "So, what do you want for supper?" Still early but thinking about their dinner was best done sooner than later, if he had to go to the supermarket.

"Can we order pizza?"

They both needed to eat. "Okay. The usual?"

"Yes, please."

Ten

St. John, New Brunswick

Serenity inserted her key card to unlock the door to her room. Five months was a long time to live out of a suitcase.

At least *Thacker, Price & Associates* didn't skimp on her accommodations. They booked her into deluxe King rooms in every city at one of the better hostelries. Still, not anything like being at home with her things.

The light on the phone blinked red indicating someone had called and left a message. Whoever it was could wait. She hauled the rolling case over to the hide-a-bed, pulled the purse's strap from her shoulder, and let it fall on the cushion. Next, she took off her coat, tossed the wool garment on the chesterfield with her bag, and kicked off her heels.

Much as she willed herself to ignore the flashing light, she walked to the desk and adhered to the sequence to retrieve the communique.

The recorded voice said, "Martin here. You've not reported in in a few days. Wanted to ensure everything was all right and you're okay."

Not having called in or emailed since the day she arrived in Saint John, she understood her boss's apprehension. At least she only had one more location to audit – Montreal. After that, prepare her proposal for the week of meetings in Québec City where she started the assignment six months before. Back then she had no problem since most of the people she dealt with were fluent in both official Canadian languages. Still, boning up on the dialect was a good idea. Here in New Brunswick, many people spoke English as their second language.

She retrieved her iPhone and tapped a short text to her supervisor assuring him all was well hoping to put his mind at rest. Until now, she communicated once a day and sometimes more often if she required something she couldn't obtain any other way.

The outlet in this city needed an update of its equipment and fixtures. Thankfully, the sales associates could work with the antique tills and make change without the benefit of a computer telling them how much to give back to the customer. In some locations, the elimination of the penny caused problems. The deficiency in math skills a contributing factor.

With its arched windows and corner doors, the place had charm. The hardwood floors creaked with each footstep.

There was no place for modern electronic tills. The workers were cheerful, hardworking and kept the store immaculate. Not a thing was out of place. Displays were neat, well arranged and after a customer created a mess, someone hustled over to make it tidy again. Serenity was quite happy to leave things as is for this location.

One of the things she admired in this branch of *jonathans* was an area dedicated to local craftspeople. Homemade candles, bath products, and other items were on sale. The space was reminiscent of the St. Lawrence Market back home in downtown Toronto. Many an enjoyable day was absorbed wandering through to see what was available, admire the workmanship the artisans put into their crafts.

Although hungry, more than food, she wanted a hot soak. She picked up her over-sized handbag and rummaged inside to find the small bag containing the citrus bombs she bought earlier. Eager to try them, and possibly acquire more before leaving if she liked them, she went into the bathroom.

Once Serenity adjusted the water to the correct temperature and put in the plug, she dropped one of the cylinders into the tub. It fizzed and foamed. Hair clipped up and undressed, she climbed in and sank into its soothing comfort.

One more full day in the city. She needed to make the most of every hour. After soaking, she perused the room service menu.

In the morning, Serenity trundled her laptop case through the door of the New Brunswick store and walked to the elevator near the back. As she entered the car, a voice called out, asking her to hold it.

A woman, about her age, hurried to the lift carrying an armload of file folders. "Cheers," she said, panting from the exertion. "Are you new here? Not seen you before."

"Not new. I'm here doing an appraisal for the head of *jonathans.* He hired the firm I work for to do a consult on the operations of all the outlets."

The other woman's face paled.

"Nothing to worry about. This store is getting a favourable rating. I love the 'old fashioned' feel to the place. Would be a shame to alter things. Sometimes, running a successful business is more than stainless steel, plate glass and computerized tills." Did she just say that? She, who wholly, believed in progress and automation. "By the way, I'm Serenity."

"I'm Melissa Scott." She shook Serenity's hand.

A firm handshake. Businesslike, not damp with nervous sweat. This lady carried herself well. At the same instant, a thought came to her. They could modernize the store and still maintain the existing appearance.

Wi-fi would connect all the computers and hide the devices under counters along with the bar-code readers. Leave the old cash registers out in plain sight. The dark-stained, tiger oak and glass exhibition cases were all in decent repair.

The vertical conveyer reached the floor housing Serenity's temporary office. She disembarked smiling. This place could be the best of old and new. Excited, she couldn't wait for her laptop to finish its boot sequence so she could add this to her notes.

This branch of the chain already had computers. They were tucked away up in the offices. Computerized till or an old manual one, you had to balance your receipts at the end of the day and put the cash in the safe.

With her MacBook Air up and running, Serenity opened her file for this shop and typed her brilliant idea. Whether her employer or the client agreed, remained unknown. She proceeded with her current focus. Depending on the cost, it might be financially viable to invest in Square registers and iPads. Those didn't function with debit cards. Previous versions of electronic card machines were currently used in the store. Newer devices that worked with chip and pin, and contactless payment, in addition to swipe, installed.

Later, Melissa turned up in her doorway. "I wondered if you fancied a bit of lunch or at least a coffee. The place across the street does good food."

The clock indicated the entire morning had elapsed. Some days her job seemed to drag. Those were consumed poring over financial statements. This morning was different. Her creativeness took over. An economic analysis needed to be done before implementing her designs. She had copies of the store's P and Ls for the last five years along with balance sheets, receivables ageing and their turnaround time for making payments. Cost out the new equipment, which would be a capital expense so taxed differently. "Sure, love to."

Coat on and cross-body bag over her shoulder, she set out. A blizzard had blown in off the Bay of Fundy. The small pellets pricked and stung Serenity's face like thousands of sharp needles. Maybe life in Toronto was all right. Not as much snow. Better transit system. Most days, she could go to and from work without ever walking more than five hundred feet at street level. The rest of her commute was underground in climate-controlled comfort.

The girls advanced into the warmth of the pub. In one of the rooms, a wood fire crackled in a gigantic fireplace. "Let's sit in here," Melissa suggested and asked the hostess if they could be seated in there.

Despite not being outdoors for long, the frigid damp air chilled Serenity to the bone. The heat emanating from the room warmed her, and they had yet to gain entry into the vaulted chamber.

While they waited for someone to seat them, they stood in awkward silence. Now they seemed to have nothing in common although they chatted like long lost friends at the office earlier.

Soon the young woman escorted them to a table and placed menus in front of them.

"Do you come here often?"

"A couple of times a month. Sometimes more." Melissa flipped through the food menu.

"You'll have to guide me."

"What do you like?"

A boyish looking girl in a T-shirt emblazoned with the name of the pub, jeans and a carpenters apron tied around her waist appeared at the table. "Can I get you something to drink to start?"

"Yes." Serenity asked for an Espresso. "One bill, please." She told the waitress then turned to her luncheon partner. "This is on me."

"But ..."

"No arguments."

Her companion ordered a coffee and smiled.

"So what do you recommend?"

"Well, the fajitas are to die for. So are the nachos. If you're not into Mexican, they do a delicious chicken burger with a boneless, skinless breast, strips of bacon, red onion, lettuce and mayo. It's one of my favourites. You have a choice of sides."

"Sold."

A few minutes later, their drinks were placed on the table. "You ladies ready?"

"Yes." She nodded to Melissa indicating she should go first.

After the waitress took her companion's order, Serenity

ordered the poultry bun with sweet potato fries for herself.

Over their beverages, they chatted.

"Tell me a bit about yourself."

"I'm originally from Ottawa. Have three brothers and a sister."

"Do you see them often?"

"I wish. The closest is my brother, Roger. He lives in Québec City. Christopher is in Alberta, Michael's in England. Amy is in Sudbury. What about you?"

"They're scattered to the four corners of the world, almost. I have no one. No siblings. No parents. To be honest, I like it that way." If Melissa only knew the whole truth. Clothes from the Salvation Army. Being razzed at school by the other students because of her outdated apparel. Money was tight most of the time, but when Erik stole the meagre amount left in the house, many days she went hungry. Her brother pulling up stakes when he did was the best thing that happened to the family.

"Really? I find that hard to believe." Melissa savoured her dark roast. "Probably times my mother wished she didn't have five of us, especially around Easter, Thanksgiving, and the festive season. Add in the out of town cousins, and we had at least ten kids running around."

Serenity cringed at the thought. Holidays were never important to her. Time off work was about all they meant. Even then, she worked from home. When she was a young girl, her parents didn't go all gooey over Christmas and Santa Claus, or Easter and the bunny. Valentine's Day didn't mean anything to them. Well, perhaps, because it was the only day of the year they didn't fight. She picked up her mug and drank.

The arrival of their food rescued her from having to answer any more of Melissa's questions. For now.

"I'm headed to Québec City in a couple of weeks after a visit to the Montreal location first. My French is atrocious, so I saved that one for the end. I'll spend my fortnight there, then follow with the week of meetings which my employer and all the store managers will attend."

"You're busy. I suppose being that way keeps you from

getting lonely."

"Are you going home for Christmas?"

"No. Not sure if I'll see any of my family this year."

In the short time she spent with the *jonathans* employee, Serenity could tell the idea of not seeing any of her relatives made her sad. "A financial thing? I'll gladly help you out, if that's the case."

"Oh, no. Not at all. Even if it were, I couldn't accept."

"If you change your mind, let me know."

Their break ended and the women returned to the store.

As Melissa went about her afternoon routine, she couldn't stop thinking about Serenity. No family. No one to share time with over the holidays. There was more to her than she shared. Still, she didn't feel right trying to pry the intimate lore from her. In the grand scheme of things, she wouldn't see her again anyway. She wouldn't accept an invitation, either. The woman was too proud. Same with her. She couldn't take Serenity's offer of money to help her go see her mother and her siblings.

Home was no longer the same now without her brothers and sisters. The last time they were all together as a family was at their father's funeral a year and a half ago. He succumbed to mesothelioma after years of exposure to asbestos. Before that, the unexpected death of her brother's wife.

Eleven

Château Frontenac, Québec City

"Get this – this thing off me." Serenity struggled to push the beast away from her. Knocked on her back, the black Lab towered over her and plastered her face with kisses. All the while, the animal's back end swayed from side to side propelled by the fiercely wagging tail.

Soon, the man caught up and got his fingers through the loop of the choker. "Bad girl, Tori." As he admonished the canine, he clipped the leather rope to the collar. "Let me help you up. I don't understand. We've let her off-leash down here in the city before, and she's never run off like this. I don't know what got into her."

The dog sat and lowered its head. A pair of doleful brown eyes projected an admission of guilt at Serenity.

"I'm Roger Scott." He reached out his hand to help her to her feet. No longer running, the fur-lined ear flaps of his red and black checkered headgear hung where they belonged, and the laces for tying them under his chin dangled. Concern-filled dark brown eyes peered from beneath the hat's fur trim covering his forehead. His dark brown facial hair was shaved short. Not a speck of grey. Eyebrows, although barely visible, likewise. No scars or other distinguishing features marred his smooth, oval shaped face.

Accepting his assistance, she took hold, and he pulled her to a standing position. "I'm Serenity. Serenity Layne."

"Can I buy you a coffee or something to apologize for what's happened?"

The boy who came thundering towards her and knocked her cheater specs over the wall tugged on the tail of Roger's parka.

"This is my son, Adam. I think he owes you an apology as well, since it's down to him your glasses went over the edge."

"I'm sorry, lady. I was trying to get them for you."

"They're cheaters so no big deal." She turned to the boy's father. "I can't accept. I'm supposed to be leading a seminar in the hotel here. Mind you, after bolting out of there; they probably don't want me back. I can't believe I was so rude and unprofessional losing my cool like that."

Gulping down a breath, she patted the dog's head. "And you …"

"Tori," said Adam.

"No more running off and knocking people down. You could have hurt me."

"Let me at least walk you to the entrance. You're not exactly outfitted for being out here in the snow."

She accepted his assistance and held his arm. With Roger supporting her, her feet still skidded on a few icy patches between the promenade and the archway.

Serenity pulled open the conference room door. "Sorry gentlemen. I forgot something back in my room." A bold-faced lie, but the best she could come up with on the spot.

Martin Thacker, nodded and mouthed, "I understand."

She shoved her hands into her coat pockets and rummaged in them hoping to find something that would back up her story. Her keychain with the red laser-like light. The appropriate gadget for pointing things out as she talked. She detached her keys and returned them to her long, brown wool outerwear before returning the garment to the hat rack in the corner.

When she took her place near the projector screen, the

troublesome store manager smirked. Miserable git. Button on the remote clicked, Serenity began. The first slides were historical facts about *jonathans* since its inception.

"You dragged us here to tell us things we already knew?" the annoying man asked.

She counted to three and breathed in. That man tried her patience right from their initial meeting in his location on Bloor Street. Because of the incident earlier in the year, she didn't audit his shop. Her colleague Phil Bradford looked after that one, and the one in the Yorkdale Mall. Since both were inside the GTA, the managers talked to one another.

"Enough. Let the woman speak," Jonathan Drake snapped and turned to her. "Continue. I'm sure we're all interested in what you have to say."

A man coming to her rescue was something to which she was not accustomed. She handled most situations with ease, but he had her so rattled, she couldn't concentrate let alone head a session.

She sucked in another deep breath and began again. "*jonathans* has been in business for over one hundred years, and I'm certain we all want to see the firm survive for another century. Those foundations keep the company going, but they're antiquated. Now is the time for the business to emerge as a model for other Canadian-owned retail chains."

Another pause. "I visited the stores across Canada, with the exception of the two Toronto locations. Another member of our agency looked after those while I travelled elsewhere. Most of them are doing well. Very well, in fact. Those successful things might not work in every location, but we can alter the positives to suit the requirements of another store."

During this portion of her talk, she kept her eyes locked on one person. He squirmed and turned crimson. She enjoyed every minute of his discomfort.

Two more hours of slides and discussions and Serenity concluded the meeting. "Thank you very much for attending today. I'll see you back here in the morning at ten sharp."

Twelve

Château Frontenac, Québec City

Serenity's clothes hung on the rail in the wardrobe inside the door. How to dress? Roger was taking her out to apologize for their disastrous first encounter. He never discussed anything about attire. Business? Casual? She was unsure what to wear and disliked those situations.

While she perused her clothing, his surname sprang to mind – the same as the woman she took to lunch in the Maritimes. The one who said she had a brother in Québec City. Couldn't be though. Scott was a common family name. The municipality stretched beyond the inner walled portion that was Vieux-Québec. Far too coincidental to be true.

In the end, Serenity chose boot-cut jeans, a long-sleeved, black T-shirt and grey blazer. She sat on the bed and pulled on her boots. She counted on there not being too much walking since her footwear had two and a half inch heels.

Her long, wool winter coat bore traces of the black Lab's attention. Stray hairs clung to it and refused to relinquish their grip on the fabric. Even an adhesive lint roller was unsuccessful.

The weather network said the temperature was minus five degrees. Snow was in the forecast.

Roger had agreed to meet her in the anteroom. When she

emerged, he stood and walked to her. His son stayed behind in one of the seats.

"I hope you don't mind Adam coming along."

The kid was there so she couldn't very well refuse. "It's fine." She was not fond of children; this one in particular. Him knocking her eyewear off the curb and over the crag did nothing to endear himself to her, even though they were cheaters. She smiled and said no more.

"Shall we?" Roger reached out his arm in invitation, and they strolled to the exit.

A gust of damp wind hit Serenity when she stepped past the shelter of the building. Happy she had her warm, wool coat, she shivered and drove her hands deeper into her pockets. She pulled out an ivory knitted beret and coordinating mitts.

As she tugged them on, she turned to her companion. "Where are we going?"

"I thought we would give you a short tour of our beautiful city. We'll stop for something to drink in our travels."

Adam started ahead of them at a run. "Come on you two. Hurry up."

She didn't own anything flat let alone winter boots. The walkway was wet, and her foot skated on an icy patch. Roger caught her before she went down. "You okay?"

Her face flushed with embarrassment. She was never this clumsy back home or elsewhere on her trip when she encountered inclement conditions. Why did she turn into a klutz when she was with him?

Once steadied on her feet, they struck out again. In front of a colossal monument, she stopped.

"Samuel-De Champlain. No one knows what he looked like, but the creator thought this would be a decent likeness based on the knowledge of the time."

At the crosswalk, Roger steered her across and down a busy thoroughfare lined on one side with boutiques and restaurants. A magnificent cathedral, the one the cab drove by taking her to the hotel, dominated the other. Further along, the roadway opened up into a bustling park. Clapboard huts, trimmed for the festive time of year crammed the space. People mingled among them.

"Our German Christmas marketplace. Opens on the American Thanksgiving and runs Thursdays through Sundays starting at eleven each morning."

"I don't know what to say." For a brief moment, the scene in front of Serenity moved her.

"I promised you a drink. We'll buy a hot chocolate from one of the vendors, and we can still walk around. There's more over there." Roger pointed to a plot on the other side. "It's prettier at night."

The aromas of fresh-cut pine and warmed cider wafted in the air. Serenity closed her eyes and tried to imagine it at night. Her well-appointed room was well within walking distance so she could visit again later after eating.

While they wandered through the maze of huts, flurries began. Fat, fluffy flakes drifted downwards. There was no wind to blow them around. In no time, this new coating of pristine white coated the dirty snow against the curbs and buildings.

Exiting the one parcel of the bazaar, they navigated to the next one. Roger found the place he wanted and ordered their cocoas. Styrofoam cups with lids in hand, they proceeded.

Adam maintained his distance in front of them. He stopped at a bench near two gypsy-like wagons and sat. Serenity joined him. A moment or two sitting to rest her feet made for a relaxing breather. The boy's father stood facing them.

"I assume you like to walk and aren't bothered by steep inclines. This city has plenty of both, and you must see the lower town."

Under normal circumstances, on flat, bare ground, heels or no heels, she loved going out for a stroll. Being in a strange place in the snow and traversing hills without appropriate footwear intimidated her. "I enjoy walking. I do a lot of it in Toronto."

"Have you been to the highest part of the CN Tower? Walked outside up there?" asked Adam.

"No."

"Sports events?"

"None of them either."

"What do you do for fun?"

The young boy's question stumped Serenity. His idea of amusement was the polar opposite to her concept. She enjoyed her career and invested many long hours in the office. The rest of her time was wasted commuting between her job and home. The word, or any related synonym, weren't in her vocabulary. Hard work, perseverance, and success were.

She didn't have a change to answer, before he asked another question. "Are you married?"

"Adam," Roger scolded.

Serenity's face seared with embarrassment. Marriage didn't enter into her plans. She had never been interested in anyone enough to contemplate such a thing. A spouse would only hold her back. No, she liked her life as it was.

"Sorry about that."

"No worries. Children are naturally inquisitive." Her lips tugged into a smile. The little toe rag. She wanted to string him up. The hairs on the back of her neck bristled.

Serenity sipped her hot chocolate. The longer they lingered, the more people arrived. "What else is there to do here besides this?"

"Plenty. If you're wearing sensible shoes or boots depending on the season. After, I'll show you a place where you can shop for some … if viewing more of the old part of the city appeals to you."

"That would be nice." Nice? What was that? She was coming unglued. Her – a workaholic, said a tour of Québec City would be nice.

After they finished, Roger ushered them along Rue des Jardins. He held her hand, ready to catch her and prevent her taking a tumble. "See over there? Nero Bianco."

Serenity nodded.

"Do you want to go now? I'll go with you, if you like."

"As long as someone speaks English, I'll be fine. I prefer to go on my own if you don't mind."

"Not at all."

Where to go? The lower town was out, even with the funiculaire to transport them up and down. Even so, it was something best done when she wore appropriate apparel. There were plenty of restaurants, bistros and pubs inside the walls of Old Québec.

He wanted to get to know Serenity better. His son in tow hindered things. At some venues, children under the age of eighteen after a certain hour were not allowed on the premises because they served alcohol.

"Would you like to go out for a proper drink this evening? Say about eight? Christianne, who lives next door could come over and keep an eye on Adam."

"Da-ad."

He shot the boy 'the look,' and the protest ended.

Roger turned to her. "Well?"

"Why not. I'd love the companionship and the prospect of seeing more of the city. You told me it was magical after dark all lit up."

"I'll pick you up at your hotel."

"I'll have sensible boots by then."

Serenity smiled as father and son walked away. The young boy, holding his dad's hand and looking up at him. What was he thinking? What was she thinking? Was Roger married? Divorced? Widowed? He couldn't be the former, could he? If he were, he wouldn't be bringing his child on dates with other women. Once they disappeared around the corner, she walked across the street.

On display was a varied selection of seasonal footwear, shoes, dress boots and handbags. A white pair with grey faux fur trim and fuzzy lining caught her eye. They also came in red and black. The light colour wouldn't stay clean long she reasoned, but then the others wouldn't either. She nudged the door open and took a couple of tentative steps over the threshold.

"Bonjour. Puis-je vous aider?" a sales clerk with long, jet-black hair, and lots of makeup asked.

What did she say? After the greeting, she didn't know what the girl said. "Hello. I don't speak French, I'm afraid."

Another associate was summoned. Relieved to be able to understand this person, a short time later, she left the store with appropriate footwear.

By the time Serenity walked out of the store, the skies had darkened. Now the lights in the trees and decorations shone brighter. She returned to the market. On her own, she could browse the various stalls and take as little or as much time as she liked at each.

Knitted goods, books, jewellery, toys, food, and an Alpine Café utilized the different wooden buildings. This time, she perused the wares at her leisure.

A chunky silver necklace, bracelet and earring set were purchased from one vendor, and a faux fur pompom keychain from another. Most of the tomes were not in English so were of no use to her since she didn't speak the language. Still, if she were to come to Québec on a regular basis, she would need to learn. A night course when she got back to Toronto ranked high on her to-do calendar.

Now, to prepare for a date with Roger. She was a nervous wreck delving into the unknown once already today. What to wear? At least put on the accessories. Fasten her keys on the fuzzy pompom keyring and link the impulse acquisition to the strap on her handbag.

Inside her room, she flung her purchases on the duvet. Her beret and mittens along with her coat topped the stack of discarded goods.

She had not been out and about long, but her feet ached. Sitting on the end of the bed, she pulled one boot off then the other. A steaming bath before going to one of the establishment's restaurants for a bite to eat would be welcome.

The long, luxuriating soak rejuvenated Serenity. Her stomach rumbled. She had gone since breakfast without food;

only the hot chocolate Roger bought in the Christmas market.

She opened the package containing the jewellery she purchased. String affixed the price tags, so she separated the strands, shoved the paper tag through the loop and removed them.

The necklace hung in the place above the neckline of her long-sleeved, black T-shirt. Bracelet slipped on to her right wrist, all that was missing were the earrings. For them, Serenity had to move to the full-length mirror beside the desk. After removing her pearl studs, she replaced them with the fishhook style hand-crafted ones.

After a quick appraisal at her reflection, she grabbed her coat, collected her purse and rushed out of her room to the elevator.

Butterflies churned in her stomach. This sensation was new to her. Never interested in boys or men for that matter, she was always too driven by her need to succeed. At work-related functions, she never went doe-eyed over any man regardless how handsome he was. Those events were work and nothing more. When up against them, she held her own. Now, she was nervous and almost giddy like the girls from her high school when they fancied a guy.

In her haste to see Roger, she forgot to make a reservation at the bistro. Luckily, she got a table, one near the window where she could look out over the St. Lawrence. People ambled by on the boardwalk over the escarpment.

Everything on the menu looked delicious. Serenity didn't want to eat a generous portion. Nor anything with pungent spices like garlic. In the end, she decided on the warm asparagus salad and a pot of green tea.

After the waitress noted her request, she tapped her fingers on the oak table. Only when she received scowls from nearby patrons, she stopped, put her hand in her lap and took in the view. The brasserie was busy, so she could have a wait before she got her food. She didn't want to have to wolf down her meal to be ready when he arrived.

Her supper came about half an hour after placing her order. At least now, she had something else to concentrate on in place of her nerves.

The salad was amazing. The lemon tarragon vinaigrette complemented the woody flavour of the asparagus and the smokiness of the bacon. The poached egg cooked to perfection, the yolk still an orangey-yellow like just cracked but cooked all the way through.

Thirteen

Roger's Home, Rue des Remparts, Québec City

Roger delayed leaving his house until almost eight o'clock. Christianne came over about seven-thirty. There was no reason he couldn't have gone sooner. Was he trying to put off the inevitable?

Not since meeting his late wife, Brigitte, all those years ago, had he dated. They courted for two years before they married. At the time of her death, Adam was seven. Three years elapsed from that time. Twelve years in total. How different from back then? What, if anything, did Serenity expect of him?

Before he left the house, he stopped at Adam's room. The kids sat cross-legged on the floor engrossed in a game of Clue. Happy games were still in favour, he smiled.

"Night, sport." He tousled his son's hair.

"You going to see her from this afternoon?"

"Yes."

"She's pretty. Are you going to marry her?"

The question took Roger by surprise. Something best ignored, although he did agree with the boy's assessment of Serenity's appearance. She was attractive. Drop dead gorgeous, but sadness brimmed over in her almond-shaped blue eyes. Someone or something hurt her in the past. Hurt was an understatement. Crushed and devastated were better descriptions. "Yes, she is pretty. No, I'm not marrying her."

He pulled Adam's door shut and leaned against the wall in the corridor. Guilt washed over him like an icy, St. Lawrence River wave. Roger scrubbed his hands down his face then laced his fingers behind his head. Maybe he should phone Serenity and call off their evening. How? He didn't have her number. Cold feet or not, he couldn't cancel.

Slate coloured wool scarf wound around his neck and trapper hat on his head, he shrugged into his black Eddie Bauer down parka. Once he was on the street, he tugged on his thermal gloves.

Since sunset, the temperature plunged at least ten degrees. The open water added dampness to the air adding to the wind chill.

They agreed to meet at her hotel. Not coming wouldn't be fair.

Rather than go inside right away when he reached the Château Frontenac, he walked over to the handrail along the walkway. Colourful reflections from the city of Lévis sparkled on the otherwise black water.

The river's shade mirrored Roger's emotions. From the time he began dating Brigitte, he never gave another woman a second glance. Until now. This wasn't cheating on his wife. Was it?

What to do?

From her table in the bistro, Serenity spotted Roger leaning on the barrier. She knocked on the window in an attempt to get his attention but was unsuccessful. All that did was draw angry looks from other diners and servers. She drained her teacup, stood, and snatched her coat from the unoccupied chair. By then, the man on the boardwalk had vanished.

Not wanting to miss him, she hurried to the exit. When she breezed into the passageway of the grand castle, he wasn't there. Let down again. The story of her life. Her disappointments came courtesy of her parents as opposed to a man, but they hurt just as much. She slumped against the wall.

Roger was different. At least she thought he was. He loved his son. Felt terrible when his dog sent her flying. He even took her for a short walk earlier in the day and arranged nighttime sightseeing under the magic of the holiday decorations.

"Sorry, I'm late."

Serenity turned at the sound of the man's voice. He looked at her apologetically. His expression reminded her of the way his black Lab looked at her.

He removed her coat from her arm and helped her into it. "There are quite a few places to go, but I think we'll go to Lower Town. We can take the funiculaire or hike down Rue de la Montagne. I think that's the finest way to take in the full effect of the beauty down there. I know a peaceful place where we can have a drink and talk. Best part is, we can hear each other and don't have to shout."

"We can walk. I don't mind now I'm wearing sensible boots." Foot raised in front of her she showed off her newly acquired winter footwear.

Nervous and unsure if he should, Roger hesitated but took her hand in his. She didn't pull back from him. That was a good sign.

He guided her to the staircase near the corner of Dufferin Terrace. "Take hold of the railing. These outside staircases can be slippery. I'll go first so if you slip, you'll have something soft to land on." Roger chuckled.

At the bridge to Montmorency Park, they still had numerous flights to work their way down until they reached the street below.

Well-lit boutique windows marked Rue de la Montagne. Their storefronts were far from Christmassy. Now they were no longer descending the steps; he retook her hand.

The sidewalk was difficult to traverse. His knees seared notwithstanding the fact he walked everywhere ... up and down hills. This was one of the steepest in the walled city.

Roger anticipated Serenity's reaction when she saw Rue Petit Champlain. The bustling confined artery was one of his late wife's favourite destinations during the holiday season. Was that why he thought about taking her here?

The road levelled off and curved to the left. Small evergreen trees afire with specks of light stood sentry along the buildings. Once past the last shop on the right, the walkway widened. "This is it. We're here." He steered her to the head of yet more flights of stairs.

Fourteen

Rue de Petit-Champlain, Québec City

Suspended overhead, snowflake-shaped lights brightened the street. Lit Christmas trees rose out of cinder blocks outside the shops and eateries. Serenity gasped. As she stood there, fluffy, white snowflakes fell. The scene, although already magical, became more so. Never had she seen such a perfect sight.

As a child in Toronto, she rarely saw a Santa Claus parade, never mind a street like this. A good number of the people in her neighbourhood were poor, scarcely above the poverty line, but some made an effort to decorate for Christmas. Not her parents, though. Her father sat in his chair in a wife-beater shirt, bottle or can of beer at his side. Most times he was practically comatose from the booze. Her mother locked herself in the bedroom unable to cope with the world.

A tear spilled down her cheek, and she dashed it away. She was tougher than that. To survive her youth, she had to be. Memories like those didn't deserve a replay. The vision in front of her was beautiful and serene. People below ambled along, part of the perfect scene. Couples held hands or strolled arm in arm. Families walked with their children.

"Shall we go?"

Roger's voice snapped Serenity out of her reverie. She

nodded. He took her hand again, and they descended the steps to the paving stone cobbles.

"You okay? You seemed miles away."

"Y-yes."

Not far down the street, a small tract stood on the right. White bulbs sparkled on a cluster of evergreen trees under an arbour festooned with pine boughs, gifts wrapped in bright paper, and Christmas baubles. Red Muskoka chairs surrounded a crackling fire pit. People chatting or checking their phones occupied most of them. An immense, crimson throne stood off to the side across from the blaze.

By now the ground wore a carpet of white. The snowflakes, far fatter and fluffier, continued to fall. Two small children scrambled into the park. They chased each other around before jostling to get to the seat.

A foreign but wistful feeling came over her. Something about being here in Québec City with this man was transforming her into a marshmallow. Her child-bearing years were coming to an end. Children were never included her plans. Her career came first. Why now?

When they reached the Italian restaurant, Roger held the door. About to step through, a tractor-trailer sped around the corner, its operator applying the engine brake to slow for the light. The powerful diesel engine's rumble changed pitch becoming louder and more menacing. The use of these, especially in this part of town, needed to be banned. They were loud, and when used, a person couldn't hear themselves think, much less carry on a conversation.

Exposed timber beams lined the ceiling. The white partitions were at least two feet thick with round-topped windows above ground level. A gas burning fireplace stood on the far wall, the fire blazing. Red colanders of various sizes, oil lanterns of the same colour, and wooden crates bordered the ledge along the foundation. Artificial Christmas greenery with berries filled in the gaps.

The host escorted them to a table near the hearthside. He

pulled out the chair for Serenity. Once she settled, the man left menus with them.

"This place is quiet, and you don't have to shout to hear yourself over the noise," Roger said.

"Lovely." She shifted in her seat.

"So what do you think of our city?"

"I love it. So, so … historical." That was a dumb thing to say. Québec was one of the earliest places to be settled in Canada. "What I meant was I'm thrilled modernization hasn't taken over."

"The advantage of being declared a heritage site. Unfortunately, it comes with a backlash. Tons of red tape and hoops to jump through if you want to do anything to your property, not to mention real estate prices are astronomical."

Everyone had their own impression of astronomic pricing. To some, the price Serenity paid for her condominium in Toronto was outrageous. Unaffordable to many. She likened housing costs in her area to those inside the wall here. Better yet, those beneath the precipice.

"You know a little about me, but I don't know anything about you other than you're staying at the Château Frontenac, and attending a conference in town. My dog could have seriously hurt you."

"Let's not go there. Not my finest hour."

"Nor mine. So tell me about Serenity."

"Isn't much to tell."

The host returned to take their order bringing their discussion to a halt.

"I'll have a Guinness. What are you having?"

"Pot of green tea, please."

"In that case, I'll have a coffee."

Unsure what to do with her hands, she fidgeted with the napkin. Roger put his on hers impeding their movement.

"You were about to tell me about yourself."

"Name, rank and serial number version … Serenity Layne, a business consultant with *Thacker, Price & Associates* on Bay Street in Toronto."

"Nothing else? What about likes and dislikes?"

She had plenty of the latter. Roger being nosey topped her list. "What about you?" She held her breath waiting for the other hoof to fall – find out he had a wife.

Their drinks arrived, and she stirred the steaming liquid in the stainless steel container. A wedding band on the ring finger of his left hand screamed married.

"I was, but I'm not now."

Unsure of what to say, she said, "Go on." If he was lying, she needed to cut her losses and escape from him at the first opportunity.

"My wife is dead. She died three years ago."

Sadness washed over Roger's eyes. He spoke the truth. No one, well almost no one, would be that cruel to lie about the death of their spouse. And convincingly. Now she felt like an idiot for asking such an insensitive question. She should have let him bring the subject up, not be blind-sided by it. "I'm sorry." Serenity took another taste.

"You didn't say much about yourself before, so come on tell me more." Roger bent forward in his chair.

"You don't want to hear about me. I told you what my livelihood is. What about you?" Personal space invaded when he shifted closer to her, she shrank back.

"Data Security Specialist at Hôtel-Dieu Hospital."

"Interesting."

Over the course of the evening, they found out more about each other but never much at one time and all work-education related. Nothing else shared.

"So, you grew up in Ottawa, got your degree at McGill, what other tidbits about Roger Scott are you willing to share?"

He smiled but said nothing.

"This is a long shot, but do you have a sister Melissa who lives down east?"

Roger's eyes widened with astonishment. "How? How do you know?" Now, he backed away from Serenity. Did he think she was some psycho or clairvoyant?

The shock of this woman knowing his sibling was evident in his mannerisms and facial expression.

"I did a review of the *jonathans* store in New Brunswick. I met a Melissa Scott there. She was quite helpful and a lovely girl. We went out to eat my last day in the town. She told me she had a brother here in Québec City. With you both having the same last name, albeit a fairly common one, I took a chance you were him."

"Not seen Mel in ages. Guess the last time would have been at …," his voice trailed off. "Dad's funeral."

"I'm sorry. I didn't mean to dredge up bad memories for you."

"No. You're okay."

They chatted and laughed over their drinks.

Roger stole a glance at his Timex. The easiest way to go back up the hill was the funiculaire. With it being after ten p.m., they wouldn't get back to catch the final ride to the peak, even if they hurried. Might as well take a leisurely stroll back to the Château Frontenac. "Shall we go? There are a couple more places down here I think you'll like."

Serenity finished her tea. When she started to put her coat on, he swept around the table and helped her.

The wind had grown stronger. The snow still fell light, and fluffy, but now instead of falling straight down, the flakes came at an angle. Despite their size, they stung on contact. Still not as bad as the freezing rain from a few weeks previous.

At the first narrow, cobbled road to the left, Roger paused. "You get a good view of your hotel from here and an excellent idea of the extent of the embankment."

"My calves and thighs are still burning from coming down that hill."

The structure stood like a gigantic castle, safe from all threats at the top of the ridge. White floodlights illuminated its exterior. Alternating green and red ones made the centre tower shine.

"It's beautiful."

"We have a fudgerie on this little street, too. Just around the corner. You must come back while you're in town."

"I will, but I'll have to remember how to get here."

"I'll be your tour guide if you like." He hoped she would accept. "In the meantime, I promised to show you Place Royale."

The huge Christmas tree in the middle of the cobbled square peeked above the mound. They drew nearer. Thousands of white mini-lights studded almost every branch. Red bows, baubles and stars adorned the rest of the evergreen. Next to it, stood a sleigh pulled by two white wire reindeer.

The city was too beautiful for words – like a fairy-tale – not that Serenity believed in them, come true. Nothing she experienced in her life compared to this. She didn't want to break down again, but long suppressed emotions threaten to bubble to the surface. No. She couldn't cry. Not here. Not now. If she found the need to, then wait until she was back in her room.

She pulled out her smartphone and snapped a photo. Mentally, she kicked herself for not taking more pictures. At least she still had more time before she had go home to Toronto.

The office would close for the day about noon on the twenty-third and wouldn't reopen until after New Year's. She had nothing or no one at home waiting for her. Why not extend her stay here? If she did, she would have to switch hotels. *jonathans* footed the bill for the duration of the meetings for his managers as well as Serenity and Martin Thacker. No way she could afford the room.

The next day was her last 'official' one in Québec City. She hated to leave. Her tour guide, albeit an accidental one, was great company, a gentleman, and knew the place well.

"I hate to have to tell you this, but we missed the last funiculaire of the night, so we're going to have to walk up the hill."

Turning to him, she said, "As long as we find another way back up that isn't as steep."

"Yes, there is." Roger took her hand and started for the dreaded Rue de la Montagne as if to climb it.

"Thank God." As she fell into stride beside him, she put her free hand on his forearm and rested her head.

"One of my favourite lanes is down this way. I can't show you the whole thing because a chunk of the cliff face broke away. They closed the road. We can go part way, but it's better done in the daylight."

Serenity smiled at Roger. She didn't mind walking. She walked every day in Toronto, to and from the subway stops, to the grocery store or the dry cleaners. The major difference was the hills. At least the Big Smoke was flat. So different from the hilly and mountainous city she found herself in now.

Overhead bridges joined the upper floors of the homes to the street. Cars filled spaces carved out of the rock face. Heavy gauge wire mesh, enveloped the rocks. Some of the properties had garages on this side. Others had built new retaining barriers and used paving stones for their parking areas. Common knowledge to Roger, Serenity wouldn't be aware. After dark, she couldn't appreciate the street's quaintness.

"I love this." She stopped and pulled her hand out of his, and turned around slowly. "Wow."

"We'll come back again in the daylight. We're almost to the point where we need to cut through the close to Rue Saint-Paul."

Roger led the way down the small laneway running between the bluff and the residences. "I know I said this was best done during the day, but this is a shorter way to the one that will take us up there." He pointed to the top of the cliff.

Serenity fell into step beside him. At the passage, Roger stood aside and allowed her to go ahead of him. The gap was too narrow for them to walk side by side.

After a short amble on the wide boulevard, he steered her to another cobbled road. The slope was nowhere as arduous as on the one they took down the hill but steep nonetheless. At least this one was more gradual. At the crest, he took them to the left up yet another incline until they reached Rue des Remparts.

Fifteen

Rue des Remparts, Québec City

Houses and small hotels aligned one side. A cramped cement walk ran adjacent to the stone fortification on the other. Roger walked to the wall. She tagged along.

"We were just down there," he said.

Serenity turned to him. "I'm glad you showed me this."

"No problem. I'm enjoying myself."

Streetlights stood at regular intervals on this side. Their round white globes lit the walkway beneath them but out from under the brightness; shadows took over.

At an observation point, Roger escorted Serenity to a bench located between two cannons. He brushed the seat off so they could sit and enjoy the scene. They were the only people out on the street. Above the rooftops of warehouses and the nearby grain elevators, the waterway was barely visible.

The snow had stopped, but the skies remained overcast, making the night seem darker than usual. Even the glow from the streetlights on either side of the area they sat in, didn't help much. Still, he enjoyed passing time with a woman and not having anything expected of him.

After their brief stop, Roger indicated they should go back to Serenity's. "With the hour, I'm going to have to take you to your hotel sooner than later. You likely have meetings, and I have work."

They scaled the hill holding hands. The further along they went, the more cannons stood guard over the city. Long-barrelled as well as short stubby weapons. The latter had carved log balls in the barrels mimicking the cast iron cannonballs from yesteryear.

Before long the Château Frontenac came into view. The centre tower bathed in alternating red and green from floodlights mounted on the edifice.

On the last part of the walk, the terrain steepened. All too soon, Roger walked Serenity through the arched street entry to the hotel. Did he kiss her goodnight? Escort her to her room? No, it would give the wrong impression. Make her think he was only interested in her for sex. The truth was, while it would be a bonus, his primary interest in her was her company and her friendship. He wished things progressed that far.

Outside, he leaned over and kissed her on the cheek. "I'll say my goodnights now. Maybe we can get together again before you go back to Toronto."

"I would like to, very much. I get the impression we've barely scratched the surface of this beautiful old town."

Roger's heart skipped a beat. She wanted to spend more time with him. At that moment, he didn't care if he was the attraction or if Québec City was.

He waited until she disappeared, then turned and proceeded down the street to Rue des Remparts and his home.

Sixteen

Château Frontenac, Québec City

Serenity tossed her coat on the bed. After she removed her
boots, she danced her way into the bathroom. What had come
over her since her arrival in this historic, picturesque town?
Couldn't be Christmas. She needed to banish that ludicrous
thought from her mind. Even as a child, this time of year was
never a big event at her house. Just another day her father got
drunk and belligerent and her mother crept off to the bedroom
helpless to cope with the situation. The part she despised most
about Christmas was returning to school after the holidays only
to hear her classmates gushing about the gifts they received.

Her evening with Roger was enjoyable. She looked
forward to spending more time with him. The feeling was
foreign to her. He was the first man for whom she felt that way.
She had plenty of male colleagues, but none of them affected
her the way he did.

She turned on the faucet and squeezed a dollop of foaming
body wash into the tub. Soon a layer of bubbles spread over the
liquid, and the lavender scent wafted on the steam. Once the
water reached the depth she desired, Serenity stripped off and
sunk into the warmth.

Even with sensible footwear, her feet and legs were sore.
The hot soak would do her the world. Traipsing around the

city, up and down hills tired her. Heels would have crippled her if she had tried to cover the distance in them.

Roger inserted his key in the deadbolt and opened the door. The rush of warm air from inside welcomed him home. Indoors, he hung his coat on the wall rack and put his keys on the hook near Tori's leash.

Curled up on the sofa under a quilt, Christianne snored. She wouldn't have settled to this extent until after Adam was asleep for the night. Not having the heart to rouse her, he let her be. She slept over before when she babysat.

When Roger turned to go upstairs, he came face to face with his son sitting on the landing. "What are you doing still up?" he asked.

"How was your date?"

"Not a date." His face burned. Yes, but not a 'romantic' one. A night out with a woman to apologize for the circumstances behind their first meeting.

Tori lifted her head and bounded down the stairs. She needed to go out one last time before the house fell into darkness for the night.

"You, into bed. I'll be back up in a few minutes to tuck you in."

"But Da-ad."

"No buts. I want you in bed when I get back from taking this one out to do her business."

Adam stood and slinked back to his room; his chin on his chest. Roger hated being firm with him. He was a good kid. Going on midnight, the young boy had school in the morning. Not to mention, he had to work the next day, too.

At the bottom of the staircase, the dog jumped and pranced. With the way Tori performed, she'd wake Christianne if he didn't soon take her outdoors. The moment he started down the steps, the black Lab raced to the back door.

If only the yard were fenced on all sides. He could let her out and go about his business while he watched for her to finish. She wandered off before. Reports of a fisher in the neighbourhood made him extra vigilant.

He clipped the leash to her collar, the loop on the doorknob, Roger slipped into his parka and out the door. Tori's snout dropped to the ground as she sniffed her way around. She would eventually decide on the 'perfect' place. Since he took Serenity back to where she stayed, the temperature had fallen. The gentle snowfall had stopped. Now the sky was clear, and the stars twinkled.

Rejuvenated after a long soak in the enormous tub, she padded to her bed and turned down the covers. Before climbing on the firm pillow-top mattress and covering up with the Egyptian cotton sheets and weighty goose down duvet, she strolled to the window.

Her room overlooked the hotel's front doors. People came and went below. The light fixtures which brightened the precinct were the same as those on the street where Roger lived.

They walked past some quaint buildings on their way back to the Château Frontenac. Was his similar?

Better yet, would she see him again? Get a grip, she told herself. Thoughts of him made her happy for the moment. When she left in a few days' time, she would be devastated.

Concentrate on business. Prepare herself for the following day.

So far the meetings had gone quite well. She dreaded the one scheduled for tomorrow. The worst saved for last, and D-Day was imminent – the Bloor Street *jonathans* location. After her experience as a customer and reading the report her colleague prepared after his audit, her first impression of the place prevailed. Now more than ever, an intervention was needed before that store dragged the entire chain's reputation down.

Her briefcase sat on the floor next to the desk. She hoisted the cumbersome thing up on her bed before turning on the bedside lamp and climbing in. The latches clicked open when she pushed the buttons. The noise seemed louder than usual, but then the room was deathly quiet. Documents for the morning get-together spread out, she drew her knees to her chest and flipped through the pages familiarizing herself with the content.

Surviving tomorrow, would be nothing short of a miracle. Bad enough, she bolted from the conference room the first day when she clapped eyes on that manager. He harassed her, and caused no end of grief and this was before she even brought up his Toronto store.

Seventeen

Château Frontenac, Québec City

"Good morning, gentlemen," Serenity said as she swept into the room exuding confidence. Too bad she didn't feel that way. Still, she had a job to do, and once she got through this day, she could return to her office at *Thacker, Price & Associates*. She turned up for the meeting last by design. She had been in earlier to set up and left the printed reports for the men. If things went according to her scheme, those in attendance would leaf through the contents of the paperwork laid out for them while they passed the time.

Her superior flashed a puzzled expression.

"There was one outlet which disappointed me. I'm not going to name names or locations, but the person knows who he is. He's a black mark on the reputation of the firm."

The man leapt from his chair, spluttering. "You can't say that about me. That's slander. I'll sue."

"Simon. Sit down and don't say another word. I should have known putting you in charge was a mistake."

He cowered and mumbled, "Yes dad."

Did she hear what she thought she heard? Simon called Jonathan Drake dad? With the elder man's comments, he was clueless as to the condition of the store. Until that moment, the familial resemblance the men bore to each other had gone unnoticed.

"I didn't perform a detailed examination at this particular location. One of my colleagues investigated. You see, the day I stopped in, for a completely different reason, I saw the way the business operated. I found it almost impossible to not 'blow my cover' before I started the investigation. If I returned after the initial encounter, I wouldn't get anywhere. Rather than jeopardize the contract awarded to *Thacker, Price & Associates*, the best course of action was to send someone else to this store."

A press of the remote button and the first slide in the PowerPoint presentation appeared. Rumpled sweaters and trousers lay on tables, more discarded on the floor beneath hangers. The same young girl who didn't seem to care if she had a job or not captured with her face down at her phone texting in another image.

Jonathan Drake's face turned crimson. Showing these pictures could cause the man to have a coronary.

"Are you all right, sir?" she asked.

He spluttered and reached for the water pitcher to fill his glass.

The whole time, his son sat unconcerned over his father's state of health; his head tilted at the man beside him talking.

The last thing she needed was to kill the head of *jonathans*. Wouldn't that look marvellous on her CV? Only a Devine intervention would keep her from losing her job. If he didn't recover, her claim to fame would be causing the head of a merchandising empire to drop dead of a heart attack.

The man's face gradually returned to a healthy glow. He appeared like he might just pull through the ordeal.

"If you're feeling up to it now, I'd like to proceed."

He waved his hand in acknowledgement and glared at his son. "Simon, you're fired," he bellowed. "Gather your things and go back to Toronto. I want you out of the business once and for all. Since you have not coughed up a cent in rent for at least a year, you and your family can move out of the house, too."

Great. Serenity got the man terminated and made homeless

in less than an hour. Conveying the state of the Bloor Street store to the attention of upper management was her only intention. "Excuse me. Can I say something?"

If Simon's evil glare could kill, she would be dead and buried. Until today, she never saw anyone this angry. Not even her father in one of his drunken rages could match this.

"I think you're being hasty, Sir." Serenity scrambled to salvage control. "I think with extra diligence and some initial supervision, we can work beyond the current situation. I mean, *Thacker, Price & Associates* are business consultants. Our job doesn't just entail efficiency audits. We can provide the guidance needed to make the Toronto outlet shine. If your son isn't comfortable with me working with him, then someone else from the agency like Phil Bradford? He did the audit of the store."

Martin Thacker stood. "Miss Layne makes an outstanding case. No one need lose their job or their home so close to Christmas. Let someone from our organization work with Simon and his staff. We. Serenity, has some brilliant ideas to incorporate into all your locations. I've seen her prospectus in its entirety. If nothing else, wait until you've viewed the plan and implementation schedule."

Relieved, she sighed. With *jonathans* being male-oriented, she was happy he intervened to be the voice of reason. She didn't see the head of the firm wanting to hear anything from her lips now.

The tension in the room eased. For the first few moments after the threat of job and home loss, the air was thick enough even a red-hot knife wouldn't cut through it. Waiting to continue, Serenity poured herself a glass of water. Her hand trembled when she elevated the vessel to her mouth. She walked to the far corner of the room to regain her composure and gather her thoughts for the continuation of the meeting.

"We'll adjourn until after lunch," her employer said. "Back to the table for one-thirty." He turned to Serenity. "You."

Her stomach lurched. She was losing her job. Tears pricked and scorched her eyes. No. She wouldn't cry here. Not in front of this roomful of men. Not until she was on her own in her room, would she let them fall.

"Get your jacket. Take a walk. Get some air. I want you relaxed to present your ideas to the *jonathans* managers. Not wound like you now are."

To her relief, Martin Thacker didn't fire her. "Thank you." Her coat was in her room, as were her new, practical cold weather boots. A break from the stuffy boardroom was welcome. With some luck she would bump into Roger. There she went again, thinking about a man she was only just getting to know.

Clad in her outerwear, beret and gloves, Serenity walked out of the lobby. Almost two hours of free time for her to wander and see more of the sights.

To her left was a small green space followed by what looked like a residential zone. To the right, her usual path when she went out was the hectic commercial section. Depending on which way she turned once through the archway, it was either Dufferin Terrace, or down the grade to the cathedral standing guard over the square.

Today, to change things up, she passed to the other side where a horse-drawn brougham awaited customers. A ride would be wonderful but something better for more than one person. Not knowing the inner city well, a walk straight up Rue Saint-Louis and back would be prudent.

Tour and transit buses, cars, and other vehicles came at her. Despite being on the sidewalk, the traffic speeding to the heart of town, frightened her. A suspension in the onslaught, due to a red light, calmed things down.

Each time a restaurant door opened, mouth-watering aromas wafted in the breeze. Outside a couple of the eateries, a hostess stood holding menus in an attempt to lure in customers.

A blast of hot air from an exhaust vent warmed her legs when Serenity walked by one of the buildings. By the time she reached the other end of the structure, gas hissed through the meter. Further up, she met another carriage carrying four people. The hollow clop of the hooves echoed off the pavement.

In no time, the wall surrounding Vieux-Québec loomed in the distance. Traffic navigated through the arched portal. At this intersection, the street was two-way travel but going from where she came, the road switched to one-way only. About to cross to walk back on the other side, something told her to stop. Tires howled on the cobbles and popped on the concrete grout between the stones. The vehicle turned across in front of her, not even slowing to make the corner.

Her heart pounded from the fright. After taking some long, cleansing breaths to calm down, she turned and walked back on the same side she was on.

"Bonjour," one of the young girls greeted as she passed by the establishment.

Serenity nodded and smiled but kept walking – concentrating on getting back to her room intact. After her near miss, she was more cautious before she moved off the curb at one of the narrow side streets.

Not far from the hotel, a storefront on the opposite side caught her attention. The window displayed soapstone carvings. A quick check to see nothing was coming the wrong way first, she looked right and when the roadway cleared darted across. Polar bears, Inuksuk's, and other Inuit art lined the sill. Inside, against the end wall, a case featured more of the hand carved sculptures.

According to her Fitbit, she had time to grab a bowl of soup before the meeting re-convened. She accessed the Bistro from the outdoor entry, welcoming the warmth and pleasant aromas.

Martin Thacker waved her over to where he sat by the floor to ceiling windows. She removed her beret and unzipped her coat before striding across the room to join him. Once Serenity reached the table, he stood and helped her out of her outerwear and into the chair opposite. "I'm glad you took my advice and got some fresh air."

"Was an experience. I love this city even if the motorists drive like lunatics. I almost got run down by a car up the street."

A waiter came with a menu and left them to carry on their conversation.

Men from the meeting sat at other tables. They conversed, sometimes loudly, over excessive lunches and glasses of draft beer.

When the young man returned with a pitcher of water, he filled the empty goblet and topped up the other.

Conspicuously absent from the group of businessmen were Jonathan Drake and his son, Simon. Were they off having a father-son tête-à-tête or a heated argument? In the short time, the two interacted in front of her; the latter was the most apt scenario.

People watching was a past time Serenity loved. She acquired her fondness for it as a child when she retreated to her room and stared out the window at the people passing. Who were they? Where were they going? The older she got, the more cynical she became. She embraced her 'new normal.' Living life on her own. No one to break her heart. She had no one to depend on and no one dependent on her.

"Are you ready to order?" the waiter asked when he returned.

"French onion soup please."

"And to drink?"

"Just water is fine."

After he left, Martin leaned forward. "Excellent job with this assignment. I'm pleased and I know the partners back in Toronto are happy, too. Don't let the man annoy you. He's an irritant. Now he's found a chink in your armour, he'll pick and pick and grind you down. The worst thing you did was run off the first day. At least you recovered well."

"I wish the incident didn't happen, too. That man walking into the conference room took me by surprise, even though I knew he was a manager. Then finding out he was the son of the head of *jonathans* – it blew me away."

A bowl of steaming soup placed in front of Serenity

interrupted their conversation. She used the moment to snatch a look at the people on the boardwalk. Between now and when she returned to the restaurant, snow had begun to fall. The promenade now wore a coat of white. The flakes fell blown in circles by the currents generated by the open water. The ferry to Lévis pulled away from the quay, and across the water, its counterpart started for Québec City.

Martin Thacker stood, bade farewell to her and reminded her the upcoming meeting started at one-thirty. "Be on time."

Serenity lifted a spoonful of melted cheese and wine infused goodness to her mouth. The soup tasted every bit as good as the aroma wafting in the air when she walked to the table. She rechecked the time. Just after one, she had plenty of time to eat in leisure. Didn't have to gulp down her meal and rush herself into heartburn of epic proportions.

Her mind drifted again, and she turned to the window. Did she expect to see Roger walk by with the dog? Better yet, did she want to see him pass? A couple of men from the *jonathans* paused near the rail. Puffs of steam left their mouths. Not until the orange glow of a lit cigarette end glowed brighter, did she realize they were smokers and getting their last one in before the afternoon session.

Lunch over, she dabbed her lips with the napkin and stood to leave. A quick stop in the ladies' room then back to the boardroom to ensure everything was satisfactory for the next meeting.

Serenity swept in full of confidence. The slimy Simon Drake wouldn't get the better of her again. Never. For this part of the series of meetings, she wished Melissa Scott was in attendance. The girl had been so helpful during the review of the Maritimes outlet and knew the demographics of that area well. Unfortunately, the young woman didn't hold a management position so wasn't invited. Still, the man who ran the store was amiable, knowledgeable and not resistant to change.

After the last of the men sauntered in, including the two

she saw on Dufferin Terrace smoking, the afternoon session commenced. The retail chain's shops ran the gamut of sleek, modern, glass-fronted buildings, to outlets in supercentre complexes to historic properties and everything in between.

"I hate to keep going back to this, but one of the Toronto stores needs a facelift." She pressed a key on the remote and brought up a photo of the Bloor Street store. "You don't need to pay a fortune doing so. A coat of paint inside and out will do wonders. Pale greys and off-whites. Either will brighten the outer facade and the interior walls. The newer buildings are designed with drop ceilings to hide the electrical, heating and cooling ductwork, plumbing and networking conduits, so you don't have much choice. That goes for all the modern stores, but you can use it to your advantage to a degree."

She clicked to the next photograph. "Demographics are different in every city. This store in Winnipeg had a marvellous array of women's swimwear when I visited their location. Who doesn't want to escape someplace tropical in the dead of winter? Look at the fun depicted. Nothing too awkward to pull the ceiling down."

"I think of all the locations I studied; my favourite one was in New Brunswick. Modernization didn't ruin the charm of the centuries-old building. Squeaky hardwood floors, the old-style cage elevator, and the creaky staircase made the place special. They're equipped to take credit and debit payments electronically but only at certain places. Secure Wi-fi and extenders at various locations will help in that respect. All traces of modern technology have been or will be cleverly hidden so to maintain this travel back in time."

Store by store, Serenity laid out her platform for conversion beginning with simple things like paint to more extravagant strains on the pocketbook.

"I noticed a couple of stains on the tiles on the top floor here. The roof needs repair, not just where the leak is but the entire thing. An inherent problem with all flat-roofed buildings, and eventually, all will need maintenance. For the outlets in malls, research your leases to see who is liable for the cost of those repairs."

She stopped for some water before carrying on. "Some of the stores have designed their own websites. They're more like blogs, but as I stated in the beginning, a secure site for your customers and yourselves is a necessity. Within it, an inventory program which will track products sold, remaining and your pre-set reorder point."

A click of the remote brought up another slide. This one showed wheel with spokes. At the ends, stars represented each of the *jonathans* outlets. "Your name has been out there for years, but you can make your business grow to even higher levels. With e-shopping, customers who don't live nearby or can't visit a physical store can still obtain your products. I had the opportunity to browse the departments in your stores during my audits. I'm impressed with the variety, the quality, and the price. You provide superior value for money spent."

"How can we do this? By building on the successes over the years create a consistent virtual presence. You need a website, and it has to be secure. A to safeguard the visitors which we expect will translate into shoppers, and B protect *jonathans* from hackers. You must adhere with the upcoming privacy changes. FTC and GDPR are coming. You have two exceptional IT people in your employ. I invited Frank to speak with you and outline the steps we're pursuing."

She chose him because he was better spoken than Derek. Either one would have done an excellent job. And if the head of the company didn't want to give up his two employees to work on the project, there were numerous reputable IT companies specializing in this.

Frank, looking decidedly uncomfortable in a suit and tie, stood. The following image was the first rough sketch he and his partner had made with Serenity. He explained the logic and the architecture required. From the blank looks on many of the faces, the managers were not sure what was in front of them.

"So there you have it. Web-based accounting software plus a WAN which will allow all the stores to talk with each other and head office. Citrix or Sysco have the hardware to make it all work."

"Thanks, Frank," Serenity said as she clicked to the next

slide.

Someone at the far end of the table applauded. "We've been trying for this for years."

She smiled. "Social media is another place where you need to have a presence. Facebook; one page for each location. Set up your sales or other events in the calendar and invite people to come out to their local outlet. Have photos of samples of your merchandise – a brief history of the business. Yes, these will be on your Internet site. However; the more you put yourself out there, the more people will see you. When they make their next purchase, *jonathans* might be the recipient of their spending."

Throat parched from speaking, she topped up her glass and took another sip before continuing. "Both Pinterest and Instagram are picture oriented which makes them great for showcasing your products. You don't have to get on to every website. These three will best fit with your image. Remember this, Facebook post's half-life is ninety minutes. A Pinterest post boasts a half-life of about three and a half months! Before I close, while your signage is distinctive, all lowercase italicized letters and no apostrophe in the name, it's time for a makeover. I believe this 'brand' has been in place about fifty years?"

Jonathan Drake nodded but remained silent.

A photograph of four different images displayed on the panel. "You don't need to decide now. Only one will adorn the *jonathans* storefronts. Which one do you like best?"

"These are too modern looking for my store," stated the manager of the Saint John outlet.

"What if you substituted the exterior LED lighting because of the historic building and district you're in, for brass letters above the front entry? The illuminated signs could be in the window openings behind the displays and done in such a way as to not overpower them. You wouldn't switch them on until closing time."

"That might just work. An excellent idea, Miss Layne."

"You're welcome. I wish you all a magnificent Christmas vacation with your loved ones." Serenity almost retched on her last sentence. She never knew a wonderful holiday season. Growing up, her Christmases were far from that. Now, on her own, at least they were peaceful. No parents were fighting. Just her, her big-screen television and selection of DVDs. "We'll get together again in the new year."

Everyone in the room except Simon Drake stood and applauded.

His father, the head of the brand, came over and shook her hand. "I have to admit at first, I had my doubts about a woman heading up this revitalization, but I'm happy to say I was wrong. You did a stupendous job."

Her employer appeared at her side during the exchange. "I told you Serenity was the right person."

"Shouldn't have doubted you, Thacker."

"I think this calls for a celebration. What do you think?" His eyes met hers.

"I'm fine. I was only doing what I was paid to do." Once she uttered those words, she rushed out of the conference room.

In her haste to escape from the room, she forgot to gather up her personal property. The corridor provided warmth and a moment or two of solitary time. Celebrating after the result of the meetings was a grand idea, but she wanted to share her wonderful news with only one person, and he wasn't there.

Should she call him at work? Obtaining the phone number of the infirmary would not be difficult. Would it make her seem desperate? Yes. Still, she needed to see him again. What if she walked to the hospital and met him? Couldn't do that. She didn't know how late he worked or the exact location of his place of employment.

The boardroom door swished forcing her to duck into an alcove. Martin Thacker and the client exited the space. Other than herself, they were the last two in the room. Once they were around the corner, she returned and collected her belongings, including her MacBook Air. As she loaded the laptop into the wheeled case, the idea of meeting Roger appealed to her even more. First, she would take her computer to her room and exchange her business attire for something casual.

Dressed in skinny jeans and a bulky-knit turtleneck sweater, she pulled on her boots, grasped her coat and handbag to leave.

"Serenity. Wait."

She turned. Her boss bee lined to her. The meetings were over. She said she didn't want to celebrate. Why couldn't he take that for an answer? Why did he use her first name? In the office, he called her Miss Layne except before the conference call at the beginning of the contract. The familiarity made her uncomfortable.

"I'm glad I caught up with you."

One more delay. In an attempt to feign interest, Serenity smiled at him.

"Just got off the phone with the other partners. They're in full agreement. After the job you did on the *jonathans* deal, the promotion is yours. The corner office and all the trimmings."

"I-I don't know what to say." A feather would have knocked her over. The announcement dumfounded her. At one time, she lived to hear those words. Now, they were no longer important.

"Say yes."

"Mr. Thacker ..."

"Call me Martin. We're partners now."

Not yet. That depended upon acceptance of the situation. "This is a huge step. Can I take a few days to consider it?" Would that appease him? Buy her some time?

"Of course. Take all the time you need as long as I have your answer when we re-open for business after the holidays."

No pressure at all then. "Er ... I want to stay here in Québec City a bit longer. Decompress after the last few months."

"You don't want to go home and celebrate Christmas with ..."

"An empty condo? No thanks." She turned to leave then

stopped. "I'll see you in the new year, and you'll have my decision by then at the latest." She didn't give him time to respond but darted out into the street.

Across Place d'Armes stood the tourist information office. They would have maps there. If unable to find his place of employment, she could meet him at his home on Rue des Remparts.

Roger mentioned his house was the opposite way to what they walked back from the town below the hill. The hospital or his residence were a great way to get out and see the city on her own.

The door at the office was heavy. Serenity struggled to pull it open. Rooms on each side of the corridor housed customer service points. To her left was a six-foot-tall statue of a snowman. In the other one, racks of brochures and, she hoped, maps of the city, took up the space creating corridors within the room. Near the entrance, a ticket machine was installed under a 'please take a number' sign written in both languages.

When her turn came, she approached the agent. "I wonder if you could tell me where to find Hôtel-Dieu." Pleased she remembered, she smiled.

The young bespectacled man's mouth gaped open. "You're not sick or injured are you?" he finally blurted out.

"No. No." Serenity assured him. "If you can provide me with a map of the city, I can make my way there among other places."

The clerk bent down and retrieved a single leaf atlas. Once unfolded, he spread it out on the counter. "You're here. The hospital is here." He circled both with a yellow highlighter.

"And Rue des Remparts?" Questions like that made her sound like a stalker asking for these specific locations, despite not giving a reason for wanting to know.

The agent traced the road in the fluorescent liquid.

"You've been a great help." She took the accordion folded paper and left the building in haste.

Soon after she ventured outside, the bells in the cathedral tower pealed. Five o'clock. Too late to meet Roger at work and tell him how the series of meetings went. Best walk down the hill past the park. Maybe meet him along the way. She was confident he didn't have a car. That meant he would be on foot or using public transit.

White spotlights shone on the red metal roof of the bistro to the right of the tourist information office. Further down, garlands graced the storefronts.

Serenity turned the other way and negotiated her way down Rue du Fort and past Parc-Montmorency. Uncomfortable walking alone on the open side of the street like the night Roger walked her to her temporary home; she kept to the side next to the structures. First was the seminary according to what she could read of the map in the glow from the streetlights.

Not wanting to make herself look like an easy mark, she fumbled to fold the page and crammed the paper in her pocket. If she carried on, she would end up where she wanted to be. After dark, being on her own walking in a strange city frightened her. The shadows cast by the intermittent light were eerie. Anyone could be lurking in them. The more these thoughts came to her, the quicker she walked.

Footsteps sounded. As they closed in they became louder. Someone shadowed her and her heart raced. Her worries were for naught. The man stepped off the sidewalk and into her peripheral vision. Eyes straight ahead, he bypassed her then returned to the walkway in front of her. Still, she received a scare. She paused and waited for the pounding in her chest to slow to normal.

After a few deep breaths to calm herself, she proceeded. By now, she had reached the cobbled road she and Roger climbed. He told her then; his house was beyond that. Some houses had the outside lights turned on and facades decorated. This segment was more residential than the previous one.

How far was she from where he lived? Did she turn around and go back? Carry on? An outdoor light provided sufficient brightness, and she pulled out the diagram. She decided two blocks and no more.

With her head down in the map, she kept going further from her starting point with each step. As she came to the first intersection, a wall of parka collided with her. She stumbled backwards but remained on her feet. The person had on a trapper hat with the flaps down protecting their ears.

"I'm sorry," she stammered. "Not watching where I was going."

"Serenity?"

"Roger?" Coincidence? Not likely. Given the time, he would be on his way home from work. Inside, she smiled. Outwardly, her cheeks grew hot from her blush.

"I should be the one apologizing to you. I almost knocked you down."

"What is it with us? First the dog now you. Do you bowl all your women over?"

"You look half frozen. Come in and get warm."

Before she agreed or refused, for that matter, he had his key out and the house unlocked. He opened one of the double, leaded-glass doors and stood aside for her to enter.

Serenity took a tentative step over the threshold into the foyer. A flight of steps with stained treads and bannister, white spindles and risers led upstairs. The door frames and baseboards were the same shade as the staircase.

Roger helped her remove her coat and hung it on the barn board rack for her then placed his own beside it. "Go on through." He extended his arm steering her to the living room.

Tori lifted her head from her bed along the far wall, stretched and trotted to where they were her tail wagging. In front of the window stood an enormous Christmas tree. It was as tall as some in the corridors of the Château Frontenac. Roger passed her and flipped the switch illuminating the thing in hundreds of coloured mini-lights. Red, blue, green, and white reflected off balls and other ornaments.

Serenity walked to the ornamented evergreen. With the effort he put into decorating, he kept Christmas alive. On a table in the corner, a portrait of a couple and a small child smiled out from the acrylic frame. She lifted the photo and took a keener look. The man and his son were with woman who had to be his wife and the boy's mother. The one who perished a few years ago.

"Would you like to stay and eat with us?"

His voice startled her, and she returned the photograph to its original location.

"I can't promise you a gourmet meal. Here at the Scott residence, Friday night is fries and fish sticks."

The mention of them made Serenity's mouth water. Those very things had been a once a week staple at her house when she was small. Quick, simple and so much better than Kraft Dinner or Habitant Pea Soup. To this day, she couldn't look at either. "Sounds delicious. Not eaten them in ages."

Roger strode to the base of the stairs. "Adam, come set the table."

A few minutes later the boy charged down to the main floor. She expected him to slide down the bannister but he didn't.

"Lay an extra place. Serenity is staying for supper."

He hurtled into another room. Soon there was a racket from the back of the house. Cupboard doors banged. Cutlery rattled in the drawers.

A rustic farmhouse table with four ladder-back seats was in the back corner of the L-shaped room where she stood. Two identical extras were in the corners framing a matching wall unit. The small boy dropped the knives and forks on the table's surface. The utensils clattered when they landed. He disappeared and reappeared with the plates.

Serenity gasped anticipating the crash of breaking China which never came. He zipped around the piece of furniture setting each place. After he vanished, she wandered to the dining area. A door swung back and forth on its hinges. The kitchen was visible in the moments the door was open. She entered. The fridge stood in the far corner, the sink along the middle of the counter under the window on the same wall. A built-in dishwasher was in the cabinets next to the double basin. The stove was on the other side of the galley.

Roger struggled to get into the bag of frozen fries.

She rushed to his aid. "Where are your scissors?"

He pointed to the drawer.

Shears in hand, she cut through the end of the plastic and poured the chips on the parchment paper-covered baking tray.

"What can I say? I'm hopeless." Roger laughed nervously.

Once they finished eating, cleared away the dishes, and loaded the dishwasher, Adam asked, "Do you want to see my room?"

"I hope it's in a fit state to show people," his father said.

The young boy had accepted her into the family.

She smiled and said, "Sure."

He jumped up from the table and took her hand. With somewhat more restraint, she stood and followed him up the stairs.

They walked by an open door. A heavily wooden-framed bed with a mattress high off the floor, overlaid in a navy duvet and bed skirt, took up the viewing slot. Coordinating shams protected the pillows.

Adam opened the door to his room. "Come on," he urged and advanced into the darkened zone.

Once Serenity reached it, he turned on the light. All things solar system decorated the interior. A mural of the cosmos plastered two adjoining walls. Matching the seams in the corner must have been a nightmare. The other two, painted dark blue, were about the same colour as the coverings in the first bedroom. A mobile of the planets hung suspended over the head of the bed. Even the bedding matched the intergalactic theme.

"Very nice. You're into astronomy, I see."

"Yes. One day I'm going to be an astronaut and go to the International Space Station." His enthusiasm gushed.

Serenity knew all too well dreams could be shattered at a pin drop. It happened to her so many times she gave up dreaming altogether. Diligence and refusing to fall into the pit of self-wallowing pity her parents inhabited got her where she was. Aspirations had nothing to do with her success. Still, she couldn't defeat the kid while his vision was so vivid. Who knew? With hard work and determination, he might just achieve his fantasy.

"I'm sure you will." She smiled at him.

"Why don't you come for Christmas?" By now Adam's excitement knew no bounds, and he jumped up and down on his bed.

"You and your father have other plans, I imagine."

"No. Say you'll come."

"I don't know. I have nothing planned for the day, but ultimately your father has the final say."

Adam stopped jumping and clambered off the bed.

"Do you want to play Snakes and Ladders? Dad and I always do on Friday night."

"Never played before."

"What?" The boy's mouth gaped open, and his eyes widened. "You don't know how?"

"No. We never had games in the house when I was growing up."

Adam raced out of the room and thundered downstairs. She went after and caught up with him as he glided across the floor on his knees to the buffet in the dining room. He rooted through a stack of boxes until he found the one he wanted.

"Can I help you?" Serenity offered. She opened the box and pulled out the board.

"What colour do you want to be?"

"Blue. That's my favourite."

"I'm always red and Dad is white." Adam put the pieces out along with the dice. "You go up the ladders and down the snakes when you land on the squares with them."

Serenity stood her piece with the other two.

By now, Roger joined them, and the round commenced. Uproarious laughter prevailed every time someone came to rest on a snake and slid back down to the beginning.

She won the first. Her face flushed. "Beginner's luck."

Come Adam's bedtime, three games were played and she triumphed and was declared the champion.

"Okay sport. Time for you to say goodnight. I'll come up to tuck you in shortly."

"Aw. Can't we play another?"

"Not tonight."

"Maybe you'll invite me again."

"Sure." He scampered away.

Roger walked her to the sectional then excused himself.

She sank into the overstuffed cushions. The dog sauntered over and sat on the floor in front of her. Tori's chin soon rested on her thigh. Not only were games of any kind missing from her childhood but pets, too. She reached over and rubbed the dog's head.

There was something about being here away from the bustle of Toronto that made her relax. She could be happy here in Québec City. Even more thrilled here in this house with him, his son and their dog. Would they want her to stay?

Soon, he reappeared with two mugs of hot chocolate. He handed one to her and eased himself to the sofa beside her then placed his on the coffee table. "It's from La Fudgerie in Lower Town."

Eighteen

Roger's Home, Rue des Remparts, Québec City

Roger bent down to unload the dishwasher. Adam sat on the counter next to the appliance swinging his legs. Each time he swung them back, his heels bashed against the cupboard doors. The noise grated on Roger's nerves. When the battering pushed him to his limit, he straightened up and clutched his son's ankles and held them to prevent them from moving. "Must you?" His tone was sharp and angry.

Teardrops welled up in the boy's eyes.

"Sorry, son. I didn't mean to snap. Just that constant pounding is doing my head in."

Adam nodded but kept silent.

After Roger returned to the task at hand, the small boy said, "I like Serenity. She's fun."

He liked her, too. This past week flew by too quickly for his liking. The chances of seeing her again, especially after she went back to Toronto and fell into a routine, were slim and none.

"Dad, can she spend Christmas with us?"

Sometimes, his son came up with incredible ideas. This was one of them. The previous night, filled with laughter and a woman's touch in the kitchen brought the house to life. Too bad, she wouldn't be the one sharing the holiday with them.

"That's a great idea, but Serenity probably already has plans."

"No, she doesn't."

"How do you know?"

"She told me."

This kid of his didn't beat around the bush. No filter on him. If he had an opinion, out it came. When did she tell Adam?

"Call her, please?"

"I don't know her number."

"You know what hotel she's staying at. Phone there."

If he didn't know better, he would swear his ten-year-old son was going on twenty. Not the small, innocent child plunked on the countertop next to him. But then, he knew that after his profile wound up on the online dating sites. Because of the slew of them, it took forever to remove himself. Still, the occasional email or text pinged his mobile. He left the room, door swinging back and forth in his wash.

Roger removed the clunky telephone directory from the drawer of the side table. He flipped through the pages until he found the listing for the hotel. Having Serenity celebrate Christmas with them would make a pleasant variation from just the two of them and Tori. Their holiday routine consisted of a tear through the gifts under the tree. Afterwards, they walked to the Plains of Abraham to play ball with the dog then back to the empty house.

The cordless handset laid on the stand. Since it was beside the base the battery might be dead. He pressed the control, and it came to life. He bent down to read the print better and dialled.

As the phone rang, he counted them. Half a dozen. "Fairmont Le Château Frontenac, how can I help you?" The female voice on the other end of the line was amiable. Her job was to be friendly, but even her tone, unlike some women's voices, was modulated and pleasant on the ears. Except for the French accent, it was as if Serenity was speaking.

"Could I have Ms. Layne's room, please? She's part of the

group holding meetings there this week." Why so formal suddenly? Why not just use her given name?

The line went dead for a moment then another phone jingled. He tapped his foot on each ring hoping she was there. If she didn't answer, he would call back and leave a message for her with reception.

"Hello," her voice sounded in his ear.

"Hi. It's Roger. Adam wanted ... I do, too, to know if you cared to join us on Christmas Day?" He sucked in a deep breath and held it while waiting for her response.

"I'm not the festive type. It was never a big deal when I was a child."

Damn. He was about to be shot down.

"But," she persevered, "I had fun with you both last night. Playing Snakes and Ladders for the first time – well, I never laughed so much in my life. I'd love to spend the day with you. Are you sure I won't be putting you out? I'm not family."

"You won't be."

"What time?"

"Earlier the better. I'm sure I can convince Adam to hold off opening his goodies until you get here. Say eightish?"

"Perfect. I'll see you then."

Serenity hung up the telephone. Presents. She couldn't just land in on Christmas Day without bringing gifts. She dashed around her room gathering her handbag, coat and boots. Dressed and ready to go last minute shopping for two people she hardly knew. Adam liked board games but she didn't want to pick up one he already had.

The elevator doors opened and she walked to the reception desk. "I'm hoping you can help me. I must purchase a gift for a ten-year-old boy. Is there a toy store here? First, I need to extend my stay. Up until now, the cost of my room has been covered by *jonathans*. I want to be here until ... " She consulted the calendar on her iPhone. "January 6th."

American Express Gold card pulled out of her wallet, she placed it on the check-in desk. She had never spent this much money on a hotel room before, but this city and this luxurious establishment were worth the added expense. Check out on the morning of the sixth and catch the train back to Toronto before returning to work on the eighth.

"Oui. Yes. We can do both. First your room then the other." The clerk booked Serenity into the same room but under her credentials. Once completed, she tore the top sheet off the pad of city maps, perused it for a moment then marked an 'X' on the location. "It's called benjo."

"How long to walk there?"

After a pause, she replied. "Between twenty and thirty minutes."

"Thank you. Merci." Serenity studied the chart for a few moments and set out with the idea of selecting a game for Adam first then something for Roger on the way back. Hopefully, both stores would gift wrap, although if she had to, she could purchase a roll of wrapping paper and tape and do it herself.

The most straightforward route was to go to the VIA station and once on that street turn left and continue until she reached her destination.

The direction you travelled made no difference to the hills in this city. At the moment, she walked downhill, but going back would be an uphill trek. A mountain goat would be hard pressed to navigate the slopes here. Still, she cherished the crisp air, the proximity to the river and the friendly nature of the people in the restaurants, shops, and her hotel. Everything here was the polar opposite of Toronto. At least before she left, she took the time to put on her 'sensible' winter boots.

At the first major intersection, after she turned on Rue Saint-Paul, an SAQ of substantial size stood to the right. Back in Ontario, the equivalent was LCBO. Even though Serenity didn't imbibe; she could get a bottle each of red and white to take with her to have with their meal. If they didn't open them Christmas Day, Roger would have it for another occasion. She made a mental note to herself to come back this way so she could stop. There was a convenience shop near her lodgings which sold wine and beer but the selection was limited and the price most likely higher.

The traffic signals flashed walk and she crossed the street. Not much further until she reached her destination now. Below the overpasses for the major highway and a couple more blocks left to go. The lack of storefronts beneath the bridges creeped her out. This was the only part of the city where she was nervous in broad daylight. Never in a million years would she walk down here after dark. Her heart pounded in her chest, and she quickened her pace to escape the shadows and parking lot. A stop at this SAQ not one of her better ideas.

Out from under the flyovers, Serenity's tension eased. She consulted the depiction again and continued to benjo.

When she approached, the sliding doors retracted. A blast of heat hit her as she stepped through the breach. A few strides further through the vestibule and she entered what a child would deem 'toy heaven' overwhelmed her. The store had something for all ages. Trucks, cars, jigsaw puzzles, babies toys, educational things. Adam loved games, so she went straight to that section. Again, the selection amazed her. Snakes and Ladders, which she knew the boy possessed, Chinese Checkers, Clue, Othello, and different versions of Monopoly lined the shelves. After much deliberation, she decided on the Ultimate Banking edition and went to the cash to pay.

Once assured Adam could exchange the game if he already had that particular version, Serenity had it gift-wrapped. She paid for it and left, the bag containing the box tucked under her arm.

Rather than go back the same way she came, she walked to the stoplights at the end of the block. Trying to pull the map out of her pocket while holding a large carton, was awkward at best. Somehow she managed to accomplish that much but, had to place the package on the ground between her feet to be able to read the chart. She was on Boulevard Charest. To the left was highway 175. If she followed that path, she would return to the heart of the downtown with relative ease.

Winded by the time she reached Rue Saint-Jean, Serenity paused to catch her breath. The last bit of the road was an uphill climb, which grew steeper the further away she got from benjo. At least this junction looked flat in both directions. Another look at her plan, and if she went away from the wall, an SAQ was within a block or two.

After a detour for wine, she started into the city. Outside of the fortifications surrounding the old part of the town, a crowd of people skated on an outdoor rink. Another thing she never did as a child. Small children wearing helmets pushed frames similar to hockey nets without the mesh as they made their way around the ice. An older girl in black leggings, sweater, and puffer vest performed jumps and spins as she zigzagged between the others. Her white fur headband, mitts and figure skates contrasted with her otherwise dark outfit.

Her parcels became more cumbersome the longer she lingered. The towering landmarks of the Price Building and Château Frontenac were invisible from this vantage point, blocked from view by hills and buildings. The name of the first cross street inside the barrier was familiar, but trekking up the steep hill didn't appeal to her. She would maintain her current route.

While she strolled down Rue Saint-Jean, she pondered a good gift for Adam's dad. As she walked by shops lining the side of the road she traversed, Serenity window-shopped. Nothing spoke to her as something he would like. Before she realized, she stood across from the flagship *jonathans* location. A eureka moment swept over her. That was the perfect place after she left her packages in her room.

The rattling of jackhammers vibrated through her feet, their thunderous noise drowning out the church bells of the nearby basilica. Once past the destruction of the structure to her right, the Art Deco edifice emerged, towering over the locality. She wasn't far from the hotel so forged onwards to Rue De Buade but instead of walking to the end, turned and walked up the narrow close. The artists were busy opening their stalls. This might be a place to get something for Roger. Although coming from here, the gift was more apt to be something for his house not him. Still, she meandered through the colourful shortcut looking at the wares on display.

Armed with this knowledge, pace quickened, in no time

she reached the Château Frontenac. In the corridor, she placed her bundles on the floor, relieved to sit them down. She swore her arms were longer after her long trip from benjo and the SAQ and back here. After unlocking her door, she retrieved the bags and schlepped into the comfort of her temporary home.

Housekeeping had been in and made up the room. Guilt washed over her as she dropped her purchases on the freshly made bed. She suffered another flashback to her adolescence. On the rare occasions her mother did housework; she didn't dare sit anything down.

After a rest stop, she donned her boots, beret, coat and mitts once more. Now was time to hunt for Roger's present. Not knowing him all that well, save for a few encounters and chats after their disastrous initial meeting, finding a gift for him would be difficult.

The plan was to go to *jonathans*. The trouble was, what was the ideal item? Shirt? Tie? Sweater? At least it had been easy to buy for Adam. She hoped he liked it. His father, on the other hand, she wanted something personal but not overly so.

More relaxed wandering the streets of the old city on her own, Serenity left her accommodations. There was more than one way she could go to reach her destination. Across the road, a horse hitched to a brougham stood tethered to a post. Another one parked on the side street.

At Rue de Trésor, the narrow lane heaved with artisans and shoppers. With the number of people milling about in the confined space, a claustrophobic person would not do well. Not that she was, but there were still way too many bodies for her liking.

Since the pathway was overcrowded, she turned so she faced the Price Building. Shops bordered the pedestrianized lane to her right. A small church occupied the space on the left, protected by a limestone wall topped with a wrought iron fence. The huts of the marketplace emerged as she approached the intersection. Maybe this would be a better spot to purchase a Christmas gift?

Serenity walked to the far end of the complex behind city hall. She meandered along the walkways between the small buildings taking in the variety of products. When she stopped to adjust her purse strap, a tall man bumped into her. She ducked to avoid an elbow.

Until now, nothing had spoken to her. In the grand scheme of things, browsing here might not have been such a good idea. Then she rounded the corner. One of the vendors had a gorgeous array of knitted goods spread out. The toques perched on polystyrene heads with scarves wound around the flexible necks, mittens and gauntlets adorned hand forms.

The only hat she was aware he owned was the trapper he wore on their evening out and their initial meeting. A red and black checkered patterned one lined with fur. One of the partial mannequins displayed coordinating neckwear. Serenity ran her hands over the yarn. The quality was outstanding, making a thoughtful but not too intimate gift along with a set of flip-top gloves in the same Buffalo Check.

"Could I get these gift-wrapped?"

After a pause, the young girl answered. "Non, sorry."

Roger's unwrapped present lie in the bag. A fur-trimmed hat-scarf combination the colour of a male cardinal's red belly caught her eye and she stroked the fur. Before leaving, she had his gift in the bottom of an oversized shopping bag with the snood, as the vendor called her acquisition on top.

On her way back to her quarters, Serenity stopped in at La Boutique de Noël. Seasonal songs played from a speaker mounted above the shop's doors. The music followed her inside courtesy of more speakers in the rafters. Everything Christmas imaginable from floor to ceiling and not a free space to be had on the shelves. Tree ornaments, fridge magnets, nutcrackers, stuffed animals among other things were on display.

At the back of the specialty shop, she found wrapping paper. Ten sheets were overkill. The emporium also stocked gift boxes, but again in packages. As it was, Serenity accumulated enough additional stuff on her time on the road.

Wistful over Christmases that never were during her formative years, she had to escape her colourful, and cheerful surroundings before she broke down in a puddle of tears. She never shared the experiences of her childhood with anyone, not even her teachers. Starting now was not an option.

Vision blurred from tear-filled eyes, she tramped back to the hotel. Why, when she never had a real family Christmas in her life, did she walk into that place?

The receptionist waved when Serenity came into the lobby. The same young woman who revealed where the toy store was and the best route to take was still on duty.

"How did your trip to benjo work out for you? The size of your bag says yes?"

"This isn't from there." She adjusted her grip. Although none of the items were weighty on their own, combined they caused the cord handles to dig into her fingers.

"You didn't find what you liked?"

"Been and back. Just back from the market, now."

"Ah. It is, how you say, a successful shop for you?"

"Very ... except for the gift wrapping."

"We can look after it for you, madam. Would you like for to leave the largesse with us?"

A wave of relief washed over Serenity. She gathered her snood then handed the rest of the parcel to the receptionist. "Just one package if possible."

"Yes. Once finished, someone will put it in your room?"

"Wonderful. Thank you so much."

Stacks of newspapers in both official languages were spread out on a table beside the check-in counter. Serenity selected a *Québec Chronicle-Telegraph*, rolled the broadsheet and turned to the elevators. When she checked out at the end of her stay, she would ensure the girl received a tip. At the very least mention her helpfulness to her manager or on Trip Advisor.

After removing her coat and boots, Serenity dropped on the bed. She settled cross-legged with the newspaper arranged in front of her. As she slowly turned the pages, the phone in her room rang. The shrill sound startled her.

About six rings shattered the silence before her heart slowed and she got to the desk where the offending object resided. "Hello," she said when she picked up the handset.

"Layne, Jonathan Drake here. I wanted to commend you on the thorough job you did for my firm."

The head of the conglomerate calling her to thank her? Strange. "I was just doing my ..."

"Nonsense. You did more than that, as you well know. I want to offer you a permanent position with *jonathans* here in Québec City. I'll match your current salary. Give you four weeks' vacation with pay right away. All benefits one hundred percent covered by the company. Plus, a substantial sign on bonus if you agree to come work for me."

Was this him or his son playing a sick trick on her? "Sir, I appreciate it. I do, but I need time to think. Picking up stakes in Toronto and moving here ... I want to make sure I'm doing the right thing."

"Of course. I understand. Give it some thought for a few days. We can discuss things further over dinner one night before you leave our city."

"Fine." She hung up. What a stupid thing to say. She rang down to reception. "Excuse me. Serenity Layne in room 325. The call that came through, did it come through the switchboard?"

"Yes. Is something wrong?"

"Can you tell me where from?"

"All I can tell you was an area number."

The line went dead. Whoever answered must have had to attend to something or someone downstairs. Local. Could have been legit. Very well could have been Jonathan Drake. Still, something about the exchange niggled at her. Did she phone the store here in town? What if the man called her from home? Even if Simon perpetrated the prank, he could have done so from Québec City.

Match her salary. Serenity doubted the man knew she drew in six-figures annually. With the promotion offered by Thacker, Price & Associates, while her remuneration continued in the same range, she would receive a substantial increase. At least she assumed she would. Four weeks' paid vacation to start. That appealed to her since it took ten years to get that many from her present employer. Not that she used much of her annual leave. Work was her life and she enjoyed her job.

However; real estate in Toronto showed no signs of slowing down. If she pulled up stakes and relocated here, she could sell her condominium for double her original investment, if not more. Allow her to pay off her mortgage and invest in a house or apartment here mortgage-free or with only a small lien against the property.

Someone impartial? That excluded her boss, the head of *jonathans*, and most importantly, Roger. If only she could talk to her parents. Seek their advice. No. The windfall was all they would see.

Phil Bradford? He did the consultation for the Toronto stores. No. Still too close to the situation. Damn! Why couldn't she think of someone? Probably, because she didn't have any friends, intimate or otherwise. She was a loner and always had been. Never opened up to anyone. What about Melissa? Only one, no two small problems. She worked for one of the stores in the retail chain and was Roger's sister.

Maybe a walk out in the fresh air would help. When she had her coat half on, the phone chirped. Was Jonathan Drake calling for an answer from her? Sweeten the pot? "Hello," she said.

"Hi, Serenity. It's Roger. Meet me downstairs."

"I was just on my way out." She fumbled with the receiver and getting her free arm into the other sleeve.

"Oh."

The dejection in Roger's voice came through loud and clear.

"I'll be right down." She hung up and finished preparing for outdoors. Did he have a sixth sense? Know she needed to talk to someone?

The last thing she grasped was her purse. She left her room putting the cross-body bag's strap over her shoulder.

The lift opened at the ground floor. Roger's beaming face made her heart flutter.

"I didn't expect to see you until Monday – Christmas Day," Serenity said when she exited the car. She had never experienced those feelings until he entered her life. Not even as an adolescent in school. The sensation, while still foreign, was far from disagreeable. In fact, she quite liked it.

With his arm around her shoulders, they stepped out into the cold. "Where are we going?" She moved her body close to his.

"Not a long way on foot that is."

On the opposite side of Rue Saint Louis, a white brougham hitched to a reddish-brown horse waited. The driver turned and waved to them.

"We're going on a carriage ride?"

They scurried across the street. The driver's bench, in addition to the interior, was red. A heart-shaped rear window rounded out the look. Helped in by the men, Serenity settled on the forward facing seat covered with a dense plaid throw. Roger climbed in beside her.

An overweight fur rug was extracted from under the front bench and placed over their laps. "Will be cold when we start moving. You'll be appreciative of it." Next, he took the blanket off his horse and stowed the animal's protective covering at the back.

"My name is Gaston, and you two are?"

"Roger and Serenity," she said.

"Ravi de vous rencontres." He shook their hands and climbed into his seat. "Lovely to meet you. Vous voulez votre visite en française ou en anglaise?"

"English, please," Roger replied.

Once they were ready to go, the coachman flicked the reins, and they lurched ahead. As they went along, the buggy swayed from side to side. The horse's shod hooves made hollow clopping sounds. The sound was more pronounced on the cobbled boulevards.

They toured past the Christmas Market, the Price Building and the only Presbyterian Church in the city. All the time, their driver sat turned facing his passengers, paying little attention to the traffic telling them about the places they passed.

When they reached Rue Saint Louis, the intersection was familiar to her. She walked here the last day of the meetings. Around the corner, another horse-drawn carriage parked next to the esplanade. They stopped for a moment, and the two drivers conversed.

An outdoor skating rink was set up on the green space. Not as fancy as the one Serenity passed before, but its function was obvious. Beyond the granite gate, a wall of plywood plastered with posters concealed a length of the city's fortifications. A wooden pedestrian tunnel protected the walkway.

Government buildings lined the street. The stately provincial legislature on their right and a newer unattractive one on the opposite side of the road.

"Up here on the left is the drill hall. Burnt down in 2008 but as you can see reconstruction is coming along well."

Murals covering the construction barrier depicted images of the building before and during the fire.

Nineteen

Château Frontenac, Québec City

Serenity woke early the morning of December 24th. Jonathan Drake's job offer niggled at her. His spiteful son could have concocted it. Sit back when she accepted it. Laugh when she found herself unemployed. Sidetracked by the invitation to spend tomorrow with Roger and Adam, she forgot.

After breakfast and showering, she decided to walk to *jonathans*. If he was not in the office – and being Sunday and Christmas Eve, he could very well be at home with his nearest and dearest. When she walked outdoors, her wet hair immediately froze, taking her back to her teen years when she left for school with her tresses dripping. How she didn't come down with pneumonia back then was a mystery, but somehow, she maintained her good health.

She pulled her snood up over her frozen hair and carried forward. A frigid breeze coming off the water blew up over the cliff and sent shivers through her entire body. At the other side of Place d'Armes, Serenity made her way to the pedestrianized section of Rue de Trésor. The confined alley between the buildings sheltered her from the wind.

jonathans was just opening for trade when she arrived. She smiled at the workforce, a number of whom she dealt with during the store's audit. The top floor housed the offices and she hurried through men's apparel to the elevator.

When she stepped out, the corridor was in darkness. She moved towards the room designated for her while she performed the consultancy. From a legal standpoint her actions questionable, but in this case, they were necessary. Serenity opened the door and hastened to the desk. The desktop computer was still there, and she pressed the power button.

As the outdated machine booted, she prayed her login still functioned. Now their business had concluded she could be removed from the network. After what seemed like forever, the sign in screen eventually popped up. She sucked in a breath and input her credentials. She exhaled once she got in. Now, she could find out Jonathan Drake's address or at the very least, his phone number.

Computer espionage and Serenity was an oxymoron. She previously had access to the majority of the records in the database. With luck the man's dossier would still be accessible to her. Bottom lip held in her teeth, she scanned through the menus until she found a heading which looked promising. When she clicked, that pull-down presented with another as did the others prior to reaching the end of the maze. There, staring her in the face, was the name, address and other information she sought. If she could hack into their network this far, they needed to beef up their security which was a high priority.

Pertinent details scribbled into her planner, Serenity backed her way out of the system, closing tabs and windows behind her and finally powering down the PC. While the computer shut off, she jammed the book into her bag. All she had to do now was get off this floor without anyone seeing her.

The stealth Gods were with her. She was out of the office, and back on the main floor unseen. She smiled again at the employees and navigated through the much busier store and out on the street.

When Serenity walked outside, snow fell in huge fluffy flakes like she was in one of those plastic globes. So much of the white stuff was in the air, the storefronts on the opposite side of the thoroughfare were just discernible, the shapes of the buildings obliterated.

Phoning Jonathan Drake and asking if she could see him was far better than landing in at his home on Christmas Eve unannounced. That was plain rude. A phone call was less apt to raise suspicions. To do anything, she had to get inside out of the heavy snow. The best place would be her room.

Back at the Château Frontenac, Serenity pulled her planner out of her purse and flipped to the page where she scribbled down the man's details. The whole time she worked on the project, she never once had to contact him there. All communications were through the store, either by phone, email or fax.

While she pondered what she would say to the man, she pulled out the map given to her. Incapable of finding Avenue St. Denis she powered up her MacBook Air. Once signed in, she opened her browser and typed the street name along with Québec City into the search box.

The man lived closer than she anticipated. Instead of turning right when she exited the entryway, if she turned left and walked to the where it ended, she came to it. Now to place the call.

She counted the rings until someone answered the phone. Finally, a woman's voice came on the line. "Hi. I'm Serenity Layne. I would like to speak with Jonathan Drake if that's possible."

The clunk of the receiver placed on a hard surface rattled in her ear. While she waited for the man to take her call, she paced around her room, nervous about the conversation.

"Drake here."

Now she felt a fool for bothering him at his home. Still, she was in this deep; she might as well dig herself in the rest of the way. "Hi, it's Serenity. I wonder if I could speak to you."

"I'm here. Go ahead."

"It-it would be better if we had this conversation in person. I hope you don't mind."

"Then you best come round. I'm at 34 Avenue St. Denis.

Do you know where that is?"

"I'll look on the computer and see you soon," she said already knowing the location of his residence.

Now that Serenity knew where he lived, she left the hotel holding the chart in front of her. She came to the route as indicated and was crestfallen when she turned the corner to a wall of rock.

A set of wood stairs spanned upward, so she trudged up them. A concrete barrier with a rickety metal rail marked the end. If this was the correct street, the one off to her right should be Rue de la Porte. She quickened her pace.

The signpost was mounted behind the high curb opposite the narrow roadway. Knowing she was in the right place, a sigh of happiness escaped her lips. Now, how much further before she reached his house? No homes were on the left side of the road. A quick consultation of the map showed it was all parkland attached to La Citadelle. The first home with identifying signage over the door was number two. He resided at thirty-four. She still had a fair hike ahead of her.

The man's home was an imposing brick mansion. The arched windows over the entrance suggested a church or at least a manse in the past. Serenity marched to the door and rang the bell.

A well-dressed, grey-haired woman, presumably his wife, answered. She wore stylish wire-framed glasses and a string of pearls around her neck. A diamond ring big enough to choke a large mammal adorned the third finger of her left hand.

Serenity swallowed hard and introduced herself. Before she crossed the threshold, she shook the snow off her coat and stamped her feet so a mess didn't get tracked in with her.

The woman opened a set of pocket doors on the right side of the opulent hallway and ushered her inside. "My husband will be with you shortly." The passage closed with a thud and Serenity was on her own in this vast room. The substantial trim and access panels retained their original stain.

A grand mahogany desk was the focal point of the room.

A banker's lamp with a green shade illuminated the polished piece of furniture. The cord plugged into a floor outlet on one side. Bookcases outlined the room. One shelf, lighted from above, housed a liquor cabinet. An antique chaise sat under the window. She perched on the edge of the seat. Was she doing the proper thing? When the man entered, she lost the time to ponder the decision.

"You wanted to speak with me, Layne." He ambled to the drinks cupboard, poured them each a Scotch, and handed one to Serenity.

"Yes, I did." She touched the glass to her lips.

"Well spit it out, woman. I don't have all day."

"Well, you know your son, and I didn't exactly get off on the right footing. I don't know how to say this, but I want to believe the deal was sincere and came from you. I don't want to find out Simon pulled a practical joke on me."

The elder Drake's face reddened. "Well, I never."

"I'm sorry, but I had to ask. If I'm to give up my job, then I need to know it's legit."

"I can assure you it is genuine. Are you accepting?"

"Not yet. I'd still like a few more days."

"Absolutely."

Serenity stood to leave. Jonathan Drake rose at the same time. She handed her glass back to him. "Goodbye. Thank you for seeing me on such short notice."

Assured the job offer was legitimate, a weight vanished from Serenity's shoulders. She loved her position at *Thacker, Price & Associates* but also embraced change. In her mind, she fist-pumped once she got outside the door of the home.

A brief consultation of the map revealed Avenue St. Denis swept around the curve. If she continued that way, she would arrive at the intersection of Saint Louis, with which she was familiar.

The name changed to Rue d'Auteuil after she rounded the corner. A row of neat terraced houses bordered the one side. The first had bright turquoise doors and window frames.

Everywhere inside the walled apportionment was nearby everything. If she were to take the *jonathans* post, she would have to find a place to live.

Affixed to the next house in the row was a bronze plaque. Taupe coloured stucco covered the exterior, and the trim was a darker shade. The varnished, round-topped, front door contained a narrow matching window.

Serenity paused outside the residence. The house was the home of René Lévesque, a former Premier of the Province, while he held the position. She took out her mobile and snapped a photo of the memorial.

The snow still fell. Not as heavy now, but the large flakes still floated down from the sky. With no other pressing business, diagram of the city in hand, and being daylight, Serenity decided to explore other areas within the fortifications.

Beyond Rue Saint Louis, an esplanade stretched along following the battlements. Houses, inns and hotels stood on the other side. Some of the homes had signs in the casements. Unsure if they said rent or sale, she could determine that at a later date.

Cars whizzed by on the cobbles. Their tires whined with intermittent popping sounds on the cracks between the stones. The first road on her right was one-way going away from her. Rather than walk down it, she proceeded straight on. Installed in the blockade was another towered gate.

From there the terrain descended in a sharp grade. With the carpet of white covering the sidewalk, Serenity determined the prudent course of action was to take another route. She crossed and went away from the wall.

Metal cladding designed to look like brick concealed the first building to the right. Perhaps granite or clay at one time, but now impossible to know. The stone structure on the left had round-topped windows, and old-fashioned light fixtures bolted to the walls. A brass plaque framed in ornate leaves was next to a red door. Not written in English, she was unable to read the inscription.

Rue Dauphine appeared flat. Serenity didn't have to put on

her best mountain goat boots to traverse the steep slopes. Scaffolding surrounded some structures. Further down, a former church morphed into a museum of literature. A retaining wall and inter-locking pavers invited people to enter the courtyard and the museum/library itself.

Serenity bucked the trend and took a cobbled pathway leading in a different direction. A metal arch adorned with pine boughs marked the entrance and exit. The top of the Price Building peeked over the roofs of the properties lining the far side of the street.

Continuing towards the landmark structure, Serenity soon found herself at the Christmas Market. Not that she needed to buy anything more, she crossed the road to wander through the stalls. She adored the quaintness of the scene.

People doing their last minute buying jostled from one stall to another. A man taller than her stomped on her instep. Her winter boots might have been excellent for walking but did nothing for the protection of her feet from clods like this guy. He didn't even utter an apology.

Until now, everyone in Quebec City was friendly. Her lack of French skills hadn't been a deterrent. She liked that. English was the language of business worldwide. What if you only spoke Arabic or a dialect of Chinese?

At least when the clod trod on her foot, she wasn't drinking a hot chocolate like the first time she visited this cheerful, holiday tract.

She paid a visit to each stall in the precinct behind city hall then moved over to the other part. Where she came from heaved with people. Over here, so many people crowded in, there was no room to move. The cloying scents of various perfumes and colognes were overpowering and took her breath away. She couldn't escape soon enough. Exit spotted, Serenity ducked under a raised arm and rushed out. On the street, she gulped down some breaths trying to suck uncontaminated air into her lungs and the taste out of her mouth and throat.

The walk back to the hotel didn't help her make a decision.

Twenty

Château Frontenac, Québec City

The glowing, red numerals on the alarm clock read four fifty-five. Too early to get up. Roger said eight would be fine. Blankets pulled over her head, she snuggled back into the cozy bed. Another hour to hour and a half of sleep was all she wanted.

What woke her so prematurely on Christmas morning? Nerves? Excitement? Both were the same thing just at opposite ends of the spectrum. Unable to return to slumber, she tossed and turned. Still, showering at this time of day and waking the other residents was rude. Just because she was awake and couldn't sleep didn't mean they were.

After flopping like a fish in a bucket of water for another forty-five minutes, Serenity hurled the covers aside. Still too soon to start running water. She could choose her outfit.

She turned on the light and heaved her massive case on the bed. Her original intention was to leave for Toronto after the meetings concluded on Friday and packed that morning. After deciding to stay in Quebec City longer, she never unpacked. Her black dress pants were neatly creased on the pile of clothing on that side of the valise. What to wear with them? The shopping bag sat on the floor under the desk.

In addition to Roger's present and the snood she purchased

for herself, she had also bought a red, hand-knit cashmere sweater. Serenity pulled out the wool pullover. Perfect with her dark trousers.

She unzipped the cover separating the compartments and took out the shoe carrier holding her shiny, ebony pumps. Outfit sorted. Selecting her clothes didn't help settle her anxiety. Before closing the suitcase, she yanked out the other items she needed, then zipped up the hard-shell and returned it to the closet inside the door.

Showered, dressed, make-up applied and hair dried, Serenity, bundle of nerves and all, was ready to make a start for Roger's house. She ensured his Christmas gift was in the seasonal, felt sack with Adam's. She had. The SAQ bag, containing the two bottles, sat beside it.

The sun rose over the water in its shades of orange, pink and red, filtered through the blue-grey clouds, created a beautiful sight. Off to the west, the skies were overcast. Billows of gunmetal-grey hung low, and the visibility was practically nil. A snowstorm had been forecast for Christmas Day, and for once, the meteorologists were right.

Serenity walked to Roger's as the church bells on both sides of the river started to chime welcoming the day. Surprisingly, many people were out and about. Some were dog walkers, others were joggers, and others, like her, toted armloads of packages in colourful wrappings.

Runners excepted, everyone else greeted her with a 'bonjour, Joyeux Noël.' Her heart soared with happiness. This was the first time Christmas was more than just another day to her. She quickened her pace.

The inclement conditions had moved in by the time she arrived at Roger's. Fat snowflakes drifted down, covering the roadways and sidewalks.

She reached for the doorbell. The young boy yelled from somewhere indoors, "Look, it's snowing!"

The door flew open before she could push the buzzer. The excited youngster stood in front of her; his mouth gaped wide.

"Hi Adam."

"Dad. Serenity's here," he hollered and disappeared back inside.

Serenity tiptoed over the threshold and closed the door behind her.

Roger appeared from the other room with Tori trotting along beside him. "Let me take these for you," he said as he removed the parcels from her hands and placed them by the archway. "You'll have to excuse Adam. He's excited. Maybe, even more this year since you agreed to join us."

Relieved of her packages, Serenity took off her boots and put on her pumps. The shoes were cold from being in just the nylon drawstring bag. The house was warm, almost sweltering.

She removed her coat and crammed her mitts and beret down the sleeve. Roger hung it on the hook and directed her into the living room. Five chairs stood around the table. Who else did he invite? She expected only the three of them. "I brought wine. I didn't know what you were serving so I got a red and a white."

A grey-haired woman came out from the dining area. "I thought I heard voices."

She was shorter than Roger and stocky but like him, her smile lit up the room.

"Mom, this is Serenity. She's the guest I told you about, and this is my mother, Lucille."

"It's lovely to meet you, Mrs. Scott." She reached out to shake the woman's hand. Roger's mother wrapped her into a warm embrace.

"My son has told me so much about you. It's as if I know you already."

Really? She didn't tell him a great deal about herself at all. Had his mom embellished to make her feel at ease, maybe? Not wanting to appear rude, Serenity returned the hug. When she pulled back, she shielded her mouth with her hand and whispered, "I didn't buy anything for your mother. I hope she's not offended."

He shook his head and said, "No."

Tori trotted to Serenity's side and pushed into her hand. She stroked the dog's head. In return, the black Lab sat and leaned against her leg pushing her off balance into Roger.

"I must get back to the turkey. You'll excuse me?"

"Sure, mom."

On their own again in the front room, Serenity breathed a sigh of relief. Roger's mother being there caught her off guard. The woman was so different from her own mother. A loving family was unfamiliar to her.

Adam charged into the lounge. "Did you bring me a present?"

"Yes."

"Don't be rude, young man."

"He's fine. I figured there was an ulterior motive behind it." She turned to him. "Yes, you may." She lowered her voice to a whisper. "One for you, too, Roger."

"Yay," the boy cheered and dove at the tree.

"Whoa down, sport. Maybe your grandmother would like to watch. Mom, Mel, come in here. Adam's dying to open his gift from Serenity."

Did he mean Melissa? Was his sibling from Saint John here, too? One unexpected guest blindsided her. But two? Normal families did come together on special occasions. Who else was here?

His sister came into the front room wiping her hands with a tea towel. "It's great to see you again. Won't hug you. My hands are greasy. Oh, I love your sweater."

Mrs. Scott came in and sat in the armchair near the hearth. Only then did Serenity notice a fire burning. No wonder the room was so warm.

"Is this the one?" Adam hoisted a large package and shook, rattling the contents.

She squatted beside him. "Yes. Now, if you already have it, you can exchange it for something different."

The festively coloured wrapping flew into the air and drifted to the floor. "Wow. Thanks. I don't have this one. Look, Dad. Ultimate Banking! Can we play now?"

"Later. After the bird is in the oven."

"Aw." Adam's chin sank against his chest.

"Tell you what, why don't you look up the rules and figure out how the game goes so when we do sit down, you can teach us?" Serenity suggested, hoping to cheer up the lad who looked on the verge of tears.

The young boy let out a whoop of excitement and tore through the plastic surrounding the box.

Roger's mother and sister started for the kitchen.

"Can I help?" she offered.

"You're fine for now, dear. But later," Mrs. Scott said.

"In that case, mom, we'll take Tori out for a walk." He turned to her. His dark brown eyes held her gaze. Her heartbeat quickened.

Outside the house, Roger steered her and the dog across the roadway. Beyond the sidewalk, the area opened up. Two long-barrelled cannons occupied a cement pad. He leaned against the wood capped battlements overlooking the city below. "I got a little something for you, too. We'll exchange gifts later once everyone else has turned in for the night."

The gesture of bringing a gift to his son deepened his feelings for her. She didn't have to do that. This was the first Christmas since before his wife died, Adam had been so happy. Thoughts of those times made him sad. Tears burned his eyes, and he spun away from her as he blinked them back.

Serenity looped her arm through his. He sucked in a ragged breath. He hadn't expected his emotions to overcome him because of Monopoly. Was he ready for another relationship?

He took her left hand in his right so she was away from the curb and they started up the street. After they rounded the corner, the pavement narrowed. He released his grip so she could precede him.

Opposite a high, modern metal-capped stone wall on the other side, he said, "This is where I work. The entire complex is hospital property," hoping to eliminate the awkward silence.

Neither had spoken since outside his house.

At Côte du Palais, Roger shortened Tori's lead and tightened his hold on it. He clutched Serenity's hand and escorted the two of them through the squirrelly intersection. He didn't know why he came this way. There were far better places to walk.

Once he had them safely across, he made a right on Rue de l'Arsenal by warehouse buildings, through a parking lot, into parkland. He unclipped the leash and the dog bounded off. Snow kicked up as she went. Occasionally, Tori turned around and barked.

"Hop on. I'll give you a piggyback ride," he said feeling playful.

"What?"

Did that mean she thought he was crazy? Maybe he was, but at that moment, it felt like the right thing to do. Or, had she never heard it referred to as that? He turned. "Well?"

"I don't know what you're talking about."

To be thirty-something and not know? "Stand behind me. Grab around my neck and jump."

Her arms looped over his shoulders. The first attempt was a failure. Serenity screamed and tightened her grip, choking him.

"Okay, not so tight."

"Sorry. Just you startled me when you reached behind my leg."

"My fault. I'll bend down a bit. Make it easier for you."

This time, things went according to plan and he had her in position. A quick boost and she shrieked.

Somewhat off balance, he started out, adjusting her weight as he went. Once, she was settled on his back, he sped up and pranced around making her squeal and laugh. Her laughter made Tori bark and she chased along beside the pair.

At the stone barrier surrounding the snow covered green space, Roger put Serenity down and fastened Tori's tether to her collar. After crossing the street, they walked through the other section of Artillery Park emerging at Rue Saint-Jean.

"I was over here the other day," she said.

"Did you go through the place?"

"No. I came down here."

"You never said."

"Well, you never asked, either."

Roger chuckled and pulled her to him then wrapped his arm around her shoulders. She leaned into him. Her standing so close revived feelings not experienced since his wife died.

In front of his house, he couldn't wait any longer to kiss Serenity. He placed his palms on the sides of her face and tipped her head back. He moved his mouth down and brushed his lips against hers. She didn't pull back which was a positive thing. Her arms encircled his waist.

It was too soon to tell her he loved her. Too soon to know for sure if he did. He was fond of her and enjoyed being with her. Love? More time would have to be spent with her to determine if his feelings went that deep.

Adam met them at the front door. "You guys were gone awfully long."

"Sorry, kiddo. Lost track of time. At least you're dressed now." Roger helped her out of her coat.

"Did you figure out the rules?" she asked.

"Yup." The boy beamed. "Can we play now?"

"My sister and your grandmother still slaving in the kitchen?"

"Yeppers."

"Maybe they'd like to join us."

"Grandma, Auntie Mel, want to play Monopoly with us?" Adam yelled as he raced to the other room.

Relieved to have a moment by himself with Serenity, Roger wrapped his arm around her waist. "You didn't think I was too forward just now."

"Not at all." She enveloped him in her arms. "You can kiss me again now if you want."

He accepted her invitation. No sooner had their lips touched than Mrs. Scott said, "I knew there was a reason for you inviting a young lady to keep Christmas with you."

His cheeks burned. Even in his mid-thirties, his mother retained the ability to make him blush.

Adam set up the game. "Aw, there's five of us, and only four can play," he pouted.

"You're fine. I need to look after the turkey anyway. You kids go on. I'll watch." She returned the fifth chair to the corner, and the others adjusted their seats and gathered around the table.

Roger picked up the rules pamphlet and read along as his son explained the nuances of using electronics instead of paper money. Aside from that, there didn't seem to be any difference between this version and the one he grew up playing.

When the kitchen door swung on Mrs. Scott's exit, the bird sat on aluminum foil on the countertop. The thing was big enough to feed a third world country, not just four adults and one child. On occasion, Serenity bought a small chicken and after cooking had meat leftover for the entire week.

After a couple of rounds of Monopoly, she excused herself. "I'll just be a minute. Mr. Real Estate Tycoon," she said directing her attention to Adam, "seems to be conducting a major property deal."

She paused before pushing through to the other room. "Are you sure I can't help with anything, Mrs. Scott?"

"You're fine, dear."

Serenity reclined against the worktop.

"Careful. Not there. You'll get your lovely clothes dirty." Roger's mother sat a huge bowl of stuffing on the counter in the location she first stopped. The woman scooped up a great dollop of the seasoned potatoes and bread crumbs and thrust it into the cavity. "My son hasn't smiled this much since before Brigitte passed away. Must be down to you."

"I don't think I can take all the credit." She folded her arms as she spoke. "Tell me about his wife. Roger told me she died."

"I don't like to speak ill of the dead, you know." She brushed an errant lock of silver hair off her face with her forearm. "She was a lovely girl but had problems." Mrs. Scott lowered her voice. "You know, those problems."

"Serenity. It's your turn," Adam yelled from the adjoining room.

She turned to the older woman. "I'm being summoned. Can we finish this later?"

An expression of resignation crossed over Roger's mother's face. There was more to his late wife's death than anyone was willing to tell.

"I'm coming." She pushed open the door. "So, what did I miss?"

"I just made a deal with Aunt Mel to buy Baltic Avenue from her so now I have the full set."

Serenity sat down and rolled the dice. She counted out the number as she moved her token, stopping on a well-developed St. Charles Place. "Who owns this?"

Roger and his sister shook their heads.

Adam smiled. "You owe me ... five thousand dollars."

"That's me finished. All my properties are mortgaged or dealt to you three, and I'm broke."

Mrs. Scott poked her head into the room. "How's the match coming along?"

"Serenity's out. She just landed on another one of my places and can't pay the rent," the young boy crowed.

"Could you put the turkey in the oven for me, please? It's too heavy for me."

"Sure, mom." He left the room and returned a few minutes later. "So Mel, do we declare Adam the winner or carry on and lose our shirts?"

Roger lowered himself to the sofa. He'd not played since he was a kid still at home in Ottawa. The truth was, he forgot how much fun the activity was. When it came to the game, his son reminded him much of himself at that age. The most significant difference back then was more people could take part at one time, and you used paper money. Serenity's choice of gift was every bit as entertaining for him.

The clatter of gathering up the Monopoly board and its related pieces floated in the air. Serenity and Mel chatted away like old friends. He was happy they got on so well. His heart warmed having at least some of his family with him. The others either couldn't afford to come home or had plans with their in-laws.

Roger didn't always agree with Brigitte's parents but not having them around, especially at this time of year hurt. His mother-in-law had cut them off without as much as a by your leave. Her reasoning was Brigitte was the only tie and severed the connection soon after her daughter's death.

Minutes later, Serenity came over and sat on the floor leaning against the sectional between his legs – hers stretched out in front of her.

"You can sit up here beside me. You don't have to hunker down there."

"I'm fine." She tipped her head back and puckered her lips in a kiss.

The dog took their actions as her cue to join them. She plunked down next to Serenity, her tail thumping the hardwood. Before settling, she stood, turned a few circles then laid on the area rug with her head in Serenity's lap.

"Tori, don't be a pain. Go," Roger said in a stern tone.

"She's fine."

In response, the black Lab snorted and snuggled closer. Even his dog was a traitor.

Adam vaulted over the end of the sofa and scrambled over to him. "Can we watch a movie, Dad?"

"What one?"

"*Home Alone?*"

Of all the movies, his son could choose, he selected that one. "Really?" he groaned.

"Don't be such a curmudgeon. I never saw it," said Serenity.

Surprised by her comment, he shook his head. With the publicity from the time of its release until now, to never have seen the show? "Go on then." He acquiesced to the choice of DVDs. His sister held no opinion on an alternative suggestion.

His mother still puttered in the kitchen. So, unless they did and were on his side, he was outnumbered.

Throughout the movie, Serenity giggled at the sight gags. Irons slamming into foreheads, hats started on fire were far from funny, but in the context portrayed, they were hilarious. He detested the nonsense.

Once the DVD finally ended, and the credits rolled, Roger puffed out a sigh. He knew all too well, Adam would want to watch the second in the series. Only a matter of time until his son swapped the discs and *Home Alone 2* dominated the television.

At least now, the aroma of the cooking poultry chucked full of stuffing tickled his nose. The bird was still a long way off from being ready but was hot enough the fragrant seasonings wafted in the air.

Twenty-One

Roger's Home, Rue des Remparts, Québec City

The words he longed to hear all afternoon rang from the kitchen. "The turkey is done to perfection," his mother announced.

Not much longer now and they would all be sitting around tucking into his mother's famous Christmas dinner.

The women went to help Mrs. Scott, with Tori in pursuit, leaving Roger and Adam on their own in the living room. The young boy, on his knees in front of the cabinet, meant only one thing. He was looking for another movie.

"Why don't you give it a rest for now." He tried to make the suggestion gentle. "Set the table or something."

After the boy trudged off, Roger tipped his head back and closed his eyes. Today was the best Christmas in many years. He dozed off thinking about the day, letting the cooking aromas channel him back to his childhood.

"Supper's ready," his mother said in his ear jolting him awake.

How long had he napped? His Timex displayed he spent well over an hour in the land of nod. Once upright, Roger stretched and ambled to the dining room table. The roasted bird lay on a platter with the carving knife and fork facing his place setting. The girls entered from the kitchen with bowls of stuffing, mashed potatoes, turnips and an enormous boat filled with gravy.

Adam scrambled into his chair on Roger's left. Mel and Serenity sat on his right, the latter closest to him, and his mother at the opposite end. Red and green Christmas crackers lay across everyone's plate.

"Can we pull them now, Dad?"

"Yes."

The young boy plucked his from both ends, and with a yank, twist, and a pop pulled the paper tube apart. The others were more subdued opening theirs. His mother and sister got hold of the strip inside and tugged. A loud snap echoed, but they still had to open the cylinder.

Serenity struggled, and he reached over and opened it for her then looked after his own. A gold crown and the riddle were the only consistent items. Each one had a unique gift enclosed. Adam got a miniature deck of playing cards. Melissa got a silver-tone pen; his mother, pierced earrings; Serenity a corkscrew in the shape of a wine bottle. His trinket was a luggage tag.

"You're the man of the house, Roger. Carving the turkey goes with the title," Mrs. Scott said.

"No pressure, bro'." She smiled and giggled.

He'd cooked whole chickens and cut them up but on those occasions, was just him and Adam. Even when Brigitte was alive, he butchered the poor beast in the kitchen, not under the scrutinization of three women.

Roger stood and picked up the carving utensils. "I make no promises." He stabbed the fork through the golden brown crispy skin into the breast.

"Can I have the pope's nose, Dad? And a drumstick."

He removed the requested parts from the bird and deposited them on Adam's plate. No need for formalities with him. With the leg off, the enormous turkey was easier for him to carve. Once sliced, he placed the pieces on another platter.

Potatoes, turnip and dressing along with the serving dish of fowl passed from one person to the next around the table followed by the gravy and cranberries.

For the first few minutes, no one spoke. They were busy savouring the feast in front of them.

"I've never eaten such a delicious dinner."

"Thank you, dear. So what do you do for a living?"

"I'm a business consultant working for a firm in Toronto. I just completed a study for *jonathans* and hosted a week of meetings going over the results."

"I met Serenity in Saint John," said Melissa.

Mrs. Scott nodded.

"Small world eh, mom?" He shoved a forkful of turkey and stuffing in his mouth.

"Dad, can Serenity come live with us?"

The statement made Roger choke and forced him to take a mouthful of water. She turned crimson with embarrassment. At least he assumed it was the reason for her blush. He was fond of the woman – exceptionally fond – but, was it far too soon to even think of living with her.

An awkward silence fell over the room. The only sounds were cutlery against China. Then the pitch changed to on glass. Melissa was standing tapping her goblet with the back edge of the knife blade. "I have an announcement to make."

"Let's have it, sis."

"I'm moving to Québec City."

"Wow, Aunt Mel!"

"What brought this on?" asked Roger. From the expression on his mother's face, she wanted to ask, but he beat her to the punch.

"Gareth and I split up." She choked back a sob.

Apparently, this fellow, whoever he was, was special to his sister. "You never referred to him in any of your emails."

"I'm having my things shipped here to this address. Hope you don't mind." She stopped talking long enough to swallow some water then continued. "Managed to wangle a transfer to the *jonathans* store here. Isn't that brilliant? Don't worry; I won't be under your feet for too long. I'm looking for an apartment, so once I find one, I'll be out of your hair."

The disclosure stunned Roger. His baby sister broken up with her partner whom he knew nothing about and now she was coming to his city. "Well done, Mel. Well not on the break up with your boyfriend, but your other news."

Melissa smiled at him and sat down.

During the silence, Serenity stood. "Since this is a day of announcements, I have one, too."

Now what? Roger took in a lungful of air and grinned at her despite worrying about what her revelation might be.

"After the last meeting Friday afternoon, my boss came to me and told me I got the promotion I wanted so badly for so long. So corner office, a personal assistant, and dare I say, a substantial pay raise. After being here and experiencing a proper Christmas …"

"I don't know how …," said Roger.

"A lot more than I ever had. Anyway, today and this last week spending time with you, your family, and your wacky dog have shown me there's more to life than a job and money."

Puzzled, he tried to work out where she was going with this statement. He didn't have long to wait.

"Jonathan Drake has offered me an upper management position. He wants me to stay on and see this project through to completion. After that, I'll be doing what I did through *Thacker, Price & Associates* but dedicated to just one firm, *jonathans.*"

Melissa squealed. "That's wonderful. We'll be working together all the time." Her excitement was apparent.

Serenity's news pleased him, too. If she moved to Québec City or the vicinity, he would be able to see her.

"I didn't say yes, yet. I told Mr. Drake I needed to think about it."

"'tis a big decision."

Serenity nodded and sat.

"What's for dessert, Grandma?"

"Pumpkin pie, fruit cake, shortbread and plum pudding."

"Can I have a piece of everything?"

"Adam." Roger's tone spoke volumes, and he didn't need to say another word.

"Pie, please."

"Finish what's on your plate first."

Dishes carried through to the kitchen and remnants scraped into the garbage, Mrs. Scott placed the China and cutlery in the dishwasher.

A fresh pot of dark roast waited on the coffeemaker. Roger took the carafe through to the dining room.

After their dessert and the table cleared, Adam brought out Monopoly Ultimate Banking again. This time Roger sat back and watched so his mother could take part.

Many hours later, they declared the tournament over, and crowned Serenity the winner.

When the house finally fell silent that night, Roger flopped on the sofa. The day had been long. Adam woke about five o'clock. Non-stop activity ensued since. He stifled a yawn not wanting to appear bored. Serenity patted his thigh and settled next to him.

The house was in darkness except for the Christmas tree. Two gifts rested unopened beneath it. The wood fire, which had blazed all day, was now only embers.

"We never gave each other our presents," he said.

"You're right. Well, come on. We'll do it now." She leapt off the couch and sat crossed-legged on the floor near the two packages. "Are you coming?"

Roger joined her. They were close enough their knees touched. He passed her the one he purchased. "Go on. You first."

She handed hers to him. "At the count of three. One … two … three."

He tore open his but didn't take out the contents. She took her time and tried to remove the tape without damaging the wrapping. "Come on already. Rip into it."

Once she did, he yanked his out of the packaging. A red and black, Buffalo Check scarf and corresponding flip-top gloves fell to the carpet.

When Serenity pulled the paper away, an identical print, hand knit item lay in her lap. She looped the sash around her neck, then took Roger's from him did the same with his. Her broad smile lit up the room. The two burst into laughter.

In a fit of giggles, she fell over backwards.

Hilarious. To think two people who had only known each other a week would come up with carbon-copy Christmas presents for one another.

"What's all the noise down there?" Mrs. Scott called out.

"Nothing mom."

The interruption was embarrassing, but Mrs. Scott's timing made the situation funnier still. He was a grown man with a son of his own, but would always be a boy to his mother. By now the couple howled, they laughed so hard.

"If you don't like your scarf, I'll return it."

"You'll do no such thing." She held it to her chest.

Roger didn't want the evening to end, but at some point, he'd have to see Serenity back to her hotel. Sure the city was safe, but now going on midnight, they both needed their rest. Him more than her. "I'll have to see you home soon."

"I suppose," she murmured.

He stood and retrieved their coats. "Come on, Tori." Kill two birds as the saying went. Escort her home and take the dog out at the same time.

Parka and trapper hat on, Roger wound his new scarf around his neck and slipped the gloves on his hands. Serenity removed her neckwear long enough to put on her wool coat then tied her wrapping. Fluorescent pink leash clipped to the dog's collar; they stepped out the door into the night.

The sidewalk was too narrow for them to walk side by side with a dog. Once they got past Côte de la Canonterie, he guided Serenity to the other side. His touch was comforting.

Today had been fantastic so unlike any Christmas day she experienced before. Giddy with excitement, she turned, so she faced Roger and skipped backwards up the street. Her actions made Tori jump and bark.

"I trust you enjoyed yourself with a portion of my family."

"I did."

They got back to the hotel too soon for her liking. "Let's

go over." She pointed to the railing.

Serenity rested her arms on the handrail. The prospect was incredible. Every night after dark, the lighting from the far shore danced on the water and each night it was different. The river's strong current altered the waves continuously. A ship sailed down river, its lights adding to the magic of the moment.

Roger propped himself on his elbow and faced her. Tori sniffed the ground and plopped beside him.

"I wanted to come back here to our 'spot.' The place where we first met. Call me a softie, but meeting you is the best thing that ever happened in my life. If not for your crazy dog." Serenity bent down to pat Tori's head. "We wouldn't be standing here having this conversation."

"Are you saying what I think you are?"

"You're more important to me than anything." She moved forward and pressed her forehead to his chest. "Until today, I didn't know what a proper Christmas was."

His hands found her cheeks, and he tipped her head back. "What do you mean?"

Serenity turned away. The embarrassment of her childhood burned her face.

"What's wrong?"

His voice, full of concern, made talking about her life more difficult. "You don't want to hear, I'm sure."

Roger led her away from the rail to one of the benches. When she sat down, Tori rested her chin on Serenity's thigh. All those years of hurt and disappointment flowed from her eyes.

"Tell me," he whispered. "I promise I won't judge." He brushed her teardrops away with his thumbs.

She took in a ragged breath. "My parents were total wastes of space. I vowed I wouldn't turn out like them. My father was a work-shy alcoholic. On the occasions he had a job, he drank most of his earnings away. My mother couldn't cope with life, and two kids, so frittered away her time locked in the bedroom. Erik, my brother, was a druggie and stole money left, right and centre from a household that had none to spare. I had one new toy, a stuffed panda bear, and he ruined it."

133

Roger's arms tightened around her. His lips touched her forehead. He had been through his own hell according to his mother. They made a great pair. Dysfunctional personified.

"Sibling rivalry, jealousy, whatever label you apply. My brothers and sisters were far from angels."

The words, while meant to be comforting, were not close to their intended purpose. Serenity straightened up and stared into his eyes. "Don't patronize me. You don't know. You'll never know." She stood and stormed back to the railing.

Two strong hands gripped her shoulders. "Come back and sit down. Tell me," he said and led her back to the bench. By now her tears flowed nonstop. "For as long as I can remember, we lived in an apartment on the top level of a house. The section of the city were one of the poorer ones, but at least the other kids had parents who were normal. They had new clothes. Okay, from discount stores but new. My stuff came from the Salvation Army Thrift Store and other used clothing outlets. They razzed me all through school."

His strong arm enveloped her, and he drew her closer.

Serenity yanked a tissue from her pocket and blew her nose. "I never had any friends growing up, so there was never any danger of bringing someone home to see the squalor. Dishes, laundry and cleaning all fell on me from the time I was a little girl. Our furniture was old and mismatched."

She twisted the single Puffs with Lotion until she ripped it to shreds. "Springs poked through the seat of the armchair my father always sat in. Our television was an old black and white cabinet model with a small rounded screen. No cable or satellite. Not even an antenna. We depended on ratty old rabbit ears that drooped all the time, so my father taped the tips to the wall will black electrical tape." She grasped the lapel of his coat and buried her face in his chest.

"Just let it go," Roger said as he rubbed her back. His upbringing wasn't perfect but compared to Serenity's, his parents were Wally and June Cleaver and life was like the 60s TV program. The house he grew up in was a modest, brick one and a half storey home on Elm Street near Booth. Some of the neighbourhood was rundown, but it was convenient for his father to go to work in Hull, as Gatineau was known at the time. He worked in the mill on the other side of the river.

The job was dirty, and years of exposure to asbestos took its toll. Mesothelioma killed the man in the end.

With the mood Serenity was in at the moment, now was not the time to talk about his formative years in Ottawa. Best to let her be. Her past, which she concealed until now, finally tumbled out. She needed to expunge the unpleasant memories from her system once and for all.

In some ways, Brigitte was the same. Kept things inside until they became too much for her to bear and then she exploded in a violent outburst. Not until the correct medical help and the right drugs were prescribed, did she maintain an even keel.

There was no comparison between his late wife and the woman he was now with. Serenity turned things around for herself and not fallen into the rut of despair her parents languished in throughout her childhood. She never said, but he assumed they died. Same with her brother, the drug addict.

Gradually, she stopped shaking. Roger twisted on the bench and raised her chin with his fingers. Mascara and eyeliner streaked her face. He brushed his lips on her eyelids and enveloped her in his arms.

In her emotional condition, he hated to leave her on her own. "Gather some things together and come back to my place for the night."

Something flashed in her eyes he couldn't read.

"I don't want you to be by yourself any longer on Christmas Day."

"But …"

"No arguments. We'll come with you. You get what you need for overnight and morning."

Serenity stood and brushed the snow off her coat. Roger wrapped his arm around her shoulders.

"What about her? Are dogs allowed?"

"I guess we'll find out."

Tori's leash wound around his hand a couple of times, and they started out for the hotel's entrance.

When they reached the room, he and his black Lab stood in the foyer while Serenity threw toiletries, nightgown, and a change of clothes in her wheeled computer bag.

About to drop the last of her accoutrements into the case, she froze. "The room is paid for tonight."

"The rest of your belongings will be here. If it makes you feel better, I'll pay."

She shook her head.

His offer, while meant in the most innocent of ways possible, didn't come out that way.

Bag packed and zipped shut, Roger extracted the handle and the two plus the dog left.

"You don't have to do this," Serenity said as they walked down the street away from the Château Frontenac. The man was sweet. He didn't want her to be by herself. She appreciated the gesture. Further proof he was a kind soul.

Neither one spoke as they made the trek back to his house. The canine, muzzle to the ground, weaved back and forth in front of them.

Could she see herself as a stepmother, dog owner, and Roger's partner? Had she read something into his invitation that wasn't there?

When they got back to his house, they tried to be quiet, so they didn't wake the rest of the family.

"You take my room. I'll sleep down here."

"I'm fine on the couch."

"No."

His voice was firm. She gave in and let him lead her up to his room.

"Bathroom is at the end of the hall," he said pointing.

He plucked the flannel pants from the footboard and disappeared. Serenity plopped on the bed. His intentions were honourable. He didn't try to take advantage. Her original assessment of him was correct. He was a gentleman.

She pulled a white cotton nightie out of her bag and changed from her street clothes into her pyjamas and padded down the hall past Adam's room.

When she passed the room Melissa and Mrs. Scott shared, a body stirred in the darkness. The last thing she wanted was to wake someone at this hour.

Back from the washroom, Serenity laid her coat on the cedar chest, clutched her sash, slid under the covers, and cuddled to her gift from Roger.

High thread-count sheets surrounded her in comfort, and the top one matched the duvet cover. The pillows were fluffy but firm.

Just as she started to drift off to sleep, the mattress lurched. Had Roger changed his mind and decided he wanted his bed? Wanted more from her than he claimed? She opened her eyes. Not him but Tori. Serenity smiled and snuggled further beneath the blankets.

Twenty-Two

Roger's Home, Rue des Remparts, Québec City

Mrs. Scott woke about five-thirty. She crept out of bed so not to disturb her daughter. Twin beds in the spare room were far more practical than the double, but Roger and Brigitte wanted the one larger bed for when couples spent the night. When his wife died, her heart ached for the pain he and her grandson went through. If the girl had only received the proper help sooner, she might not have taken her life.

Adam's bedroom door was closed and latched. Roger's was ajar. He must have been the one who flashed by the door in the middle of the night.

She tiptoed down the stairs trying to be noiseless so she didn't waken anyone. When she entered the living room, a blanketed figure stirred. Melissa was upstairs. Whoever this was, was too big to be Adam.

The woman carried on to the kitchen and started a pot of coffee. The hinges on the door creaked. When she turned, Roger stood in the opening.

"What are you doing up so early, mom?"

"I could ask you the same thing." She pointed the mug she'd retrieved from the upper cabinet at him, asking if he wanted one. After she placed it on the counter, she pulled another out for him. He took them in one hand and the milk from the fridge with the other, then walked through to the dining room.

After the dark roast brewed, she carried the thermal carafe to the table and poured. "You and Serenity were up quite late last night."

"Yeah. Sorry if we woke you."

"Is there anything you want to tell me?"

"Like what?" Roger fidgeted with his coffee mug.

"Are things serious between you two? If so, how come you never said anything before?"

"I only met her a week ago."

Mrs. Scott stood and went back into the living room. She removed the duvet from the unoccupied sectional and folded the eiderdown. She turned to her son, holding the blanket in her arms. He was hiding something from her. After raising five children, she knew when one of them was less than truthful.

She tapped her foot on the floor and waited for him to open up.

"Serenity spent the night."

"Was that so hard?"

"I'm not a little boy, mom. I'm a grown man." He rose and strode to her, plucked the coverlet from her grasp, and returned it to the end of the sofa. Hand on her elbow, he guided her to the table.

"What you do with your life is up to you, but you have a son to think about."

"Adam thinks the world of Serenity. You saw that at dinner yesterday."

"I just hope she's more stable than your wife." She clutched the cloth napkin and wrung the serviette in her hands.

Roger stirred his coffee. Pale streaks formed as the cream blended in with the chestnut brown coloured liquid. "When I took Tori out for the last time, we walked her back to her hotel."

"That was nice, but why did you bring her back here to stay the night?"

The things Serenity told him on the boardwalk adjacent to the Château Frontenac, she said in confidence. Something in his mother's tone bothered him. Was she prying because she could? Genuinely interested in her? He scrubbed his hands down his face and gulped a mouthful of the dark roast. "Yesterday overwhelmed her," he said, keeping his head down.

"Never had or been to a family Christmas before?"

If his mother only knew she hit the nail dead on its head. Serenity's story about her childhood still dumfounded him. He didn't think she'd lie to him but no one lived like that did they? Sure, poor people lived in his neighbourhood in Ottawa, but they did their best for their children. Gave them some sort of Christmas even if it was courtesy of a Salvation Army food voucher and the angel trees in the malls. "Actually, she ..."

"She what?" Serenity stood near the end of the sofa arms folded across her chest. "What all have you said?"

He needed to find a way out of the mess. Done the wrong way, he'd only dig himself deeper into the hole he fabricated. Didn't speak, but stayed quiet and strode across the room. When he reached her, he drew her close to him. "I didn't say anything," he whispered, "except you being overwhelmed, but mom was asking. When she came out with you not ever having a family Christmas, I almost fell off my chair."

Her arms encircled him. Her cheek rested against his shoulder. His shirt grew damp. She was crying. He rubbed her back to comfort her, but she stiffened and broke out of his embrace. Now what? He didn't think he'd done anything wrong.

His mother took Serenity aside and sat her at the table. Roger sank on the couch. Their voices reached him, but they were low enough he couldn't make out what they said. He stood and walked to the dining room.

Not that he was trying to eavesdrop, but his coffee was getting cold. He scooped up his mug and shouldered open the door. There was more force than intended and it into the cupboards. Roger extended his arm preventing another crash on the next swing and slowed the motion. He braced himself against the countertop and took some deep breaths. He had to get a grip. Lukewarm coffee didn't help. He poured the last of his brew down the drain and put the empty cup in the dishwasher.

About fifteen minutes later, his mother's voice drifted into the kitchen. "Can you come here?"

This time he didn't barge through, but took his time.

"Serenity wants to talk to you. I'll make myself scarce." She winked and nodded when she walked by him.

Roger sat across the table from her and took her hands in his, unsure he wanted to know the outcome. Her piercing blue eyes, red from crying, shook him to the core.

"This past week since meeting you and spending time with your family have been amazing. I mean it."

"They have for me, too."

"I told your mother everything."

"I'm glad."

"I think I'm falling in love with you, Roger Scott."

His heart skipped a beat. The declaration took him off guard. "And me with you," he added. Not phrased the way he intended, but the message came through. He loved her, too.

"I wanted you to be the first to know. I'm giving up my position at *Thacker, Price & Associates*. I'm taking Jonathan Drake up on his offer."

"I'm contacting my employer and telling him I'm not accepting the promotion. I don't want the job. I know he'll try to persuade me to reconsider, but my mind is made up."

He held her hands and stroked the backs with his thumbs.

"I met with him Christmas Eve, and we discussed things in detail. At first, I thought his slimy son Simon was playing a prank. I needed to know the *jonathans* proposition was genuine."

"Naturally."

"Not said yes, yet, but I'll be doing so straight away, too."

Roger leapt to his feet and scrambled around the table. His chair toppled over backwards and clattered on the hardwood floor. He swept Serenity into his arms, planted a kiss on her cheek then pulled back and repeated the action, this time on the lips. When their mouths separated, he whispered, "You don't know how happy your news has made me." He kissed her again.

"Now there are still some logistics to work out. I need to sell my condo in the city, and locate a property here."

"Move in with us," Adam piped up.

Heat rushed to Roger's cheeks. He had to be as red as Serenity was earlier. His son's youthful enthusiasm knew no bounds. As much as he wanted to continue seeing the woman, he couldn't bring her into his home – his and Brigitte's home. That would be cheating on his late wife. He couldn't do that. If they were to live under one roof as a family, they would find a new place together. Their home.

"I'm going to have to go back to the hotel now. Job offer to accept and a resignation letter to write, and I'm afraid if I leave things any longer, I won't do it at all."

"Let me walk you there."

"No. I won't be much company. I'll be writing in my head."

"Come back later?"

"If you'll have me." She left the room and reappeared within moments with her bag and her coat over her arm.

Roger helped her into the garment and wound her scarf around her neck. Dressed for outdoors, he walked her to the front door and kissed her goodbye.

Serenity pushed into her room. Everything remained the same from the previous night. She removed her outerwear but kept on the pashmina. The message written in her head all the way from Roger's house to the Château Frontenac. Now was the time to open her mail program and type it.

Dear Mr. Thacker,

This isn't a decision I've come to lightly.

She hesitated. No matter how many times she went over the termination in her mind, when she placed her fingers on the keyboard, she froze.

Please accept this as my letter of resignation. I appreciate everything you've done for me over the

*years at Thacker, Price & Associates, but in my time
in Québec City, I've discovered there is more to life
than working. No, it isn't the romance of the town.
I've not taken leave of my faculties. It's not my
biological clock ticking, either.*

*I want more than nine to five (most nights later)
and sometimes seven days a week. When I return to
Toronto, I'll work my notice period. My last day will
be January 26th.*

Again, she stopped. Did she mention *jonathans*
headhunted her at the end of the meetings? No. That was like
rubbing salt.

Don't try to change my mind. It's made up.

She hit the backspace and deleted the last two sentences
then typed her name, even though her email had a signature.

Her finger hovered over the mouse prepared to click
'send.' Within seconds of her sending it, her iPhone would
ring.

Courage summoned, she clicked. As predicted, her
smartphone chirped, but she ignored the incoming call. Instead,
she phoned Jonathan Drake using the room's telephone. She
accepted the position, but she wouldn't be able to start until
January 29th.

Those tasks done she moved on to selling her
condominium and searched realtors in the GTA. When she
found one, she thought capable of doing the job for a fair price,
she emailed them and added the contact details in her phone.
Being December 26th, Boxing Day, the soonest the transaction
could begin was Wednesday.

Twenty-Three

Roger's Home, Rue des Remparts, Québec City

Melissa walked into the living room carrying a steaming mug of hot chocolate in each hand. The kitchen door swung on its hinges in her wake.

Roger sat on the chaise portion of the sectional aiming the remote control at the television – the image continually changing. He didn't acknowledge her even when she stepped in front of him and placed steaming cup on the coffee table.

"We're a right pair. Sitting at home on New Year's Eve," said Melissa.

"Single father life. I'm used to staying in at night. You can go out if you want."

"What, and leave you here moping on your own? Not a chance." She sipped her cocoa. "Hey, this stuff is yummy. Where from?"

"From La Fudgerie in Lower Town."

Seated on the opposite end of the couch, she curled her leg underneath the other one. "So why aren't you and Serenity doing something tonight? I'm here, so Adam's not alone." She leaned closer to her brother.

"She's not into holidays. Planned on a quiet night in."

"If you ask me, she enjoyed herself with us at Christmas."

"Yes, she did."

"Then phone her." Melissa raised her voice as she spoke.

Tori lifted her head from her bed. Roger turned and glared at her.

"Oops. Sorry." She giggled then turned serious. "If you don't call Serenity. I will."

"At ten-thirty at night. No."

"Then walk up there and quit being such a misery guts."

A knock on the front door followed by Tori's barking interrupted their banter. Roger rose from the sectional before the dog barked the house down. "Shush," he commanded. The black Lab stopped instantly but hovered next to him.

Being on her own for a moment allowed Melissa to take custody of the remote control. She hit the guide button and searched the directory for something to watch. Her brother's choice of programs left much to be desired if he kept it on a single channel long enough.

"Someone for you," he said.

"Hi, Mel. I missed you."

She spun around. "G-Gareth. What are you doing here?"

"I came to see you. Try to make up for being a daft ape."

"Well, I can see you two have some catching up to do. Maybe I will go see her."

Roger left his sister and her ex-boyfriend to their own devices and shrugged into his Eddie Bauer parka. He pulled his plaid headgear on and grabbed his Christmas neckwear from Serenity off the rack.

Outside, he breathed a sigh of relief. He loved Mel, but the sooner she found a place to live other than with him, the happier he would be. His mother returned to Ottawa the day after Boxing Day. He pushed his hands into his coat pockets and brought out his heavy gloves.

At this time of night, he couldn't phone Serenity. Calls at this hour tended to mean bad news. Winding his scarf around his neck another time, he started up the street to the Château Frontenac. About halfway up the road, he paused and took out his cellphone. Why not? The worst thing he'd wake her up and she'd be furious with him. He phoned the hotel's switchboard and asked for her room.

When the call went through, her phone rang at least ten times, but she never answered. Roger continued toward the hotel. The New Year's Eve festivities on Grande Allée would be well underway and only a short walk up Rue Saint-Louis to the wall.

The faint strains of music wafted in the night breeze, blown down from the celebrations. As he converged on Dufferin Terrace, he spotted her leaning against the barrier, at what she called 'their spot.' Her red Buffalo-check scarf fluttered in the wind. His heart swelled with happiness at the sight, and he picked up his pace.

In order to surprise her, he turned at the sidewalk in front of Musée du Fort which pointed the way to the crest of the knoll. From here, he could approach without her seeing him. Many people were out tonight. Some meandering along the promenade, others, like Serenity, looking out over the river. Lévis on the opposite shore was well-lit. Some bright colours, some regular shades of street lamps made their reflections on the water appear magical.

"So this is your idea of a quiet night in." He encircled her waist with his arms and planted a soft kiss on her cheek.

Startled, Serenity jumped. "I didn't expect to see you tonight."

"Me either. Maybe a phone call at midnight to wish you a happy new year and that was it."

She turned around to face him and placed her hands on his forearms before resting her head on his chest. Pleased Roger had decided to venture out after all. Curious why the sudden reversal in arrangements, she asked.

"Gareth turned up on my doorstep. I thought I'd give him and Mel some space."

"Extremely thoughtful of you. They do need to talk. When she mentioned their breakup, I saw how devastated she was. I hope they can work things out."

"I do, too. She's my baby sister, and I want her to be happy."

The devotion Roger showed his youngest sibling warmed Serenity's heart. Feelings like that for her brother didn't exist. She didn't care if he was alive, dead or clean. Now she was with the one person who was important to her.

"Let's take in the New Year's Eve festivities up the street," he suggested.

"What's going on?"

"You'll see."

"Tease." She slapped him with her sash and took hold of his hand.

Many people walked to the city wall. Only after they rounded the curve in the road was the dazzlingly lit Ferris wheel visible. Serenity gasped.

"You've not seen anything yet. Grand Allée is shut down to traffic. All the bar and restaurant patios are open."

"Really? Seems a wrong time of year for outdoor terraces?"

"They have heaters."

The closer they got to the old city's rampart, the more people crowded the pavement. At times, they had to walk on the asphalt to get around the masses. Fragrant aromas wafted out the doors of the restaurants lining the street whenever a door opened tantalizing her taste buds. Music blared from exterior speakers.

Before they reached the gate, the din became overpowering. Serenity clutched Roger tighter. With a crowd this huge, getting separated was conceivable. As if he understood her apprehension, he drew her close to him. When he did, she put her arm around his waist. Together they were inseparable.

"Do you want to go on the Ferris wheel?"

Serenity shook her head. She never went on a midway ride in her life. This one petrified her. The huge ring was stopped to let passengers off, and other ones on. The idea of being in the seat at the top when stationary scared her to death. Its height was dizzying. What if a bolt fell out and the gondola crashed to the ground?

By the time they squeezed their way up the street to the National Assembly, midnight had almost arrived. Roger stopped them there. Serenity didn't question him. Québec was his city, and he knew what he was doing. Standing in front of Place George-V they turned facing the building under restoration just as the countdown to 2018 began.

Soon the fireworks started. Flashes of blazingly coloured light exploded in the sky accompanied by loud bangs and pops. The starbursts continued into the night. Roger turned her to face him. He placed his hands on her cheeks and whispered in her ear, "I love you, Serenity Layne."

Those were the words she longed to hear from him. When the *jonathans* contract began, entering a relationship wasn't part of the bargain. But she had and better still; he loved her. "I love you, too, Roger Scott." Tears moistened her eyes.

He brushed his lips against hers. Serenity put her arms around his waist and pulled him close all the while returning his kiss. Oblivious to the crowd surrounding them, the only fireworks she was aware of were those in her heart. The only other person there with her was him.

Epilogue

Gare du Palais, Québec City

On the morning of January 6th Roger, Adam, and Tori accompanied Serenity to Gare du Palais. The day dawned dull and gloomy and matched her mood.

They walked into the station with her as far as possible with the dog. The oily tang of diesel fumes from idling engines hung in the air and caught in the back of her throat.

"Don't go," said Adam. Tears filled the little boy's eyes. "I don't want you to leave."

She squatted in front of him. "I have to go, but I'll be back at the end of the month. I promise."

He wrapped her in an embrace and buried his face in her collar. She returned his hug. His emotions brought hers to the surface.

When she stood, salty tears blurred her vision. His eyes were moist, too. At this point, she didn't want to board the train. She longed to stay with them but, she promised to come back and work her notice period. She always kept her word.

Roger held her tight, bent down and kissed her. When their lips touched, she put her arms around his neck.

A shrill whistle and the 'all aboard' command separated them. Serenity snatched up her bags and ran to the coach. The conductor lifted her luggage up for her. She turned around and waved to Roger and Adam. After boarding, she wrestled her large case into the rack near the doors and took her computer bag with her. With Wi-fi available, she could continue with the project for *jonathans* on the journey home.

Serenity slumped into a seat. Her mind wasn't on work. She opened her MacBook and started a property search for a place to live in Québec City instead. She had listed her home right after Boxing Day, and had some nibbles. If she wanted to be Jonathan Drake's neighbour, there was an apartment in the stone building next door to him. No way. That was too close for comfort.

A few of the properties spoke to her, and she noted the realtor's site and address. Some were mere blocks away from Roger. They would be near enough to see each other, yet have their own space. Exposed beams and stonework walls were high on her must-haves.

"What do you mean, you're leaving the firm?" Martin Thacker spluttered and tossed a file folder on her desk. The papers within spilled out over it.

Serenity stood. "I believe I made my intentions clear in my letter of resignation."

"But the job you did on the *jonathans* contract."

She couldn't tell him she would complete the remainder of the assignment as an employee of the company which contracted the agency. "I'm sorry, my mind is made up. You won't change it." She swept around the desk and held the door open. "Now if it's all right with you, I have work to do."

The man left, muttering and shaking his head.

These next three weeks were going to be a living hell. Sever all ties with *Thacker, Price & Associates* right away? Cut and run and not put in her notice period?

January 26th would not come soon enough.

Powerless to concentrate, she called her realtor. She had booked a showing for that afternoon, but they should be out by the time Serenity got home from work. At least something was going right.

She composed an email to Roger and asked him to look at a house a couple of blocks from him.

Number 8 Rue Ste Famille. Thanks.

Close with two x's for kisses? Too forward? In the end, she typed them.

Not that it was a concern; parking was an issue in the old part of Québec City. She didn't have a car. In Toronto, she never needed one. The public transit system was more than adequate. In time, she'd learn the routes and schedules in her new hometown, too.

The rest of the day dragged on. Serenity was delighted when five o'clock came. For the duration of her employment with *Thacker, Price & Associates*, she planned on leaving on time every night, not working from home, and not going in much ahead her scheduled start time.

She packed up her MacBook Air and some of her other personal things. Rather than take them all on her last day, removing a few each night was far more natural.

Serenity paced from her office to the elevator. The car arrived before her boss had a chance to speak with, no scream at, her over her decision.

Exiting the building, she breathed in the city air. Even with the pollution, Toronto smelled better in the cold weather. It was like the snow muffled the pungencies.

Sadly, the subway didn't. The odours of food and sweat permeated the carriage. As always she ended up standing with her nose in someone's stinky armpit. The return to street level, welcoming.

Serenity turned the key in the deadbolt. A sliver of light glowed beneath the door. The realtor must have forgotten to turn off one of the fixtures. Or, she was still showing the property and extolling the virtues of residing in this trendy borough.

She pulled her rolling computer bag into the foyer behind

her. The room was deserted. No one was in the kitchen either. Still, someone was inside. Boots removed and slippers on, she moved slowly around the living room.

Before going any further, she grabbed an overweight sculpture off the coffee table. If someone were in her home, they'd regret it.

On tiptoes, she crept down the corridor towards the bathroom. The clear glass shower doors prevented anyone from hiding there. A shuffling sound came from her bedroom. She took a deep breath and flung the door open.

Her tatty panda bear wasn't in its customary place in the chair. A man stood in front of the dresser with his back to her.

"Don't move. I've called the police." The threat was empty. She hadn't dialled 9-1-1, but the intruder didn't know any different.

He turned around and faced her.

"My God, Erik. What are you doing here?"

Also by Melanie Robertson-King

A Shadow in the Past (currently under revision)
(4RV Publishing)

The Consequences Collection
Tim's Magic Christmas
The Secret of Hillcrest House
Shadows From Her Past
YESTERDAY TODAY ALWAYS
Cole's Notes (Revised version)
It Happened on Dufferin Terrace
(King Park Press)

Forthcoming (also from King Park Press)
A Shadow in the Past (second edition)

Cole's Notes (A Short Story)
EFD1: Starship Goodwords – a cross genre anthology
(CARRICK PUBLISHING, 2012)

Future Titles in the *It Happened* Series
featuring the Layne and Scott families

It Happened at Percé Rock

It Happened in Gastown

It Happened in Niagara Falls

MELANIE ROBERTSON-KING

https://melanierobertson-king.com

Melanie Robertson-King has always been a fan of the written word. Growing up as an only child, her face was almost always buried in a book from the time she could read. Her father was one of the thousands of Home Children sent to Canada through the auspices of The Orphan Homes of Scotland, and she has been fortunate to be able to visit her father's homeland many times and even met the Princess Royal (Princess Anne) at the orphanage where he was raised.

www.ingramcontent.com/pod-product-compliance
Lightning Source LLC
Chambersburg PA
CBHW052139170626
46812CB00004B/1504